BLACK COFFEE

Daniel Ford

SEPTEMBER SKY PRESS

Black Coffee

© 2019 by Daniel Ford

For permission requests, write to the publisher, addressed "Attention: Permissions Coordinator," at the address below.

50/50 Press, LLC
140 Quay Road
Delanson, NY 12053
http://www.5050press.com

ISBN-13: 978-1-947048-45-4

Cover design by Jonathan Lee
All photo credits: Cristina Cianci
Edited by: Stephen Hall III

Printed in the U.S.A.

For Cathy, who encouraged my storytelling

For Stephanie, the best story of all

Praise for Black Coffee

"Disquieting, thought-provoking, and uncomfortably honest, these brilliantly evocative stories will haunt you far past the final pages. Full of insight and empathy, and revealing a dark unsettling wisdom, these bleak, multi-layered tales are the proof of a brave new voice in fiction."—Hank Phillippi Ryan, nationally best-selling author of *Trust Me*

"In this extraordinary collection, Daniel Ford gives us a slew of unforgettable tales that reveal the grotesque, delightfully wicked facets of humanity. *Black Coffee* is filled with characters that live in memory. A writer of uncanny insight and compassion, Ford has given us a wise and poignant book. It should not be missed."—Phoef Sutton, Emmy Award-winning screenwriter and author of the *Crush* series.

"Crafted by a deft hand, imparting both narrative sympathy and brutal honesty, Daniel Ford's *Black Coffee* explores and examines a range of dysfunctional characters, all down, out, or teetering on the edge. These tales are woven at times meandering, at times taut to the breaking point, and always with a keen eye into the depths and darkness of the human psyche."—Steph Post, author of *Miraculum* and *Lightwood*

"If you're the kind of person who still can't help crying four lines into Paul Simon's 'America,' then the protagonists in

Black Coffee are bound to sing to you as well. You can't help getting lost in these stories—each one a nighttime bus ride down the Jersey turnpike, filled with love, heartache, and inescapable loneliness. But Ford also brings his own brand of dark, off-kilter comedy. He's an expert at mining humor out of despair. *Black Coffee* is a sensational collection full of unforgettable characters."—Spencer Wise, author of *The Emperor of Shoes*

"You will want to gobble up these stories and swallow them whole. With this fresh, provocative collection, Daniel Ford digs into the truth and all of the uncomfortable, revealing, unsettling, wry, twisted, gripping layers that come along with it. From dark and disturbing to smart and hopeful, Black Coffee will keep you fixed on what happens next, and thinking about all of it long after you've turned the final page."—Nicole Blades, author of *Have You Met Nora?*

"Running the complete gamut of emotion, from darkly funny to utterly heartbreaking, *Black Coffee* packs one hell of a punch. In this masterful short story collection, Daniel Ford expertly mines the human condition to reveal profound, and sometimes painful truths about loss, love, and trying to find your way in a broken world. It's also an insightful and revealing meditation on masculinity. It made me laugh and cringe and cry. I absolutely loved it!"—Bianca Marais, author of *Hum if You Don't Know the Words* and *If You Want to Make God Laugh*

"What a sweet pleasure it is to be in the hands of a gifted young writer with a whole mess of empty pages in front of him. Daniel Ford's stunning, stirring story collection, *Black Coffee*, is like the best cup of Joe—heady, crisp, piquant, and filled with the promise of good things to come."—Daniel Paisner, author of *A Single Happened Thing*

"A love of coffee isn't the only thing linking this finely crafted exploration of human connections. You'll find stories that move with ease from violence to touching, from funny to heartfelt, all written with masterly prose. Author Daniel Ford has created a stunning collection."—Edwin Hill, author of *Little Comfort* and *The Missing Ones*

"With this collection of stories, Daniel Ford establishes himself as a modern-day Charles Bukowski. Tinged with alcohol, sex and, oftentimes, violence, these gritty tales take us to coffee shops, bars, and other similar settings where people come together at random to take a break from and sometimes lock horns with life. And at the core of each of the characters who inhabit these stories is a bit of inextinguishable hope fueled by the prospect of love, friendship, or family. I suspect you'll read these more than once, which is the greatest compliment I can give them." — Drew Yanno, author of *The Smart One* & *In the Matter of Michael Vogel*

"Ford's title story begins, 'I remember darkness. Never total. Never complete. Just enough to provide nightmares.' Which aptly sums up the broken characters who populate this riveting collection. Regular people trying to struggle, fight, claw, and love their way through the darkness. Often stumbling, sometimes falling. But always, always searching for the light."—Giano Cromley, author of *What We Build Upon the Ruins* and *The Last Good Halloween*

"*Black Coffee* is like riding public transit through an entire city. Each new stop opens a door to the distinct voices of those who are trying to make it. At times, ill-mannered, racy, and lost; you'll love learning from the characters who enter and exit with you."—Calder G. Lorenz, author of *One Way Down (Or Another)*

"These are stories about what comes after, be it war, joy, or heartbreak. What happens to those who carry others only to be left without support of their own? What's left when we're left to ourselves? Ford's stories, sly and sardonic, search for the answer."—Grayson Morley, winner of the 2018 PEN/Dau Short Story Prize for Emerging Writers

"Daniel Ford's stories twist and unsettle, but most surprising is the wit and warmth he finds in the darkest corners." — James Tate Hill, author of *Academy Gothic*

"*Black Coffee* is the work of a vivid, rousing, committed, and agitative imagination. Dive in and enjoy the thrilling, intoxicating, jarring ride. The stories here are spectacular and positively gripping."—Gary Almeter, author of *The Emperor of Ice Cream*

Contents

Introduction

I met Daniel Ford about five years ago at my first real job. At the time, he was working on his first novel, *Sid Sanford Lives!* That work, like most writers' first novels, goes a long way to understanding Ford's writing style and its amalgamation of pain and hope borne from a middle-class New England upbringing. The novel is bursting at the binding with pain and sweat and blood. Ford's characters are constantly ramming their bodies and minds against the concrete tides of New York City. Their struggle quickly endears them to the reader. But once they have taken hold of you, Ford does everything in his power to dash them against the pavement, over and over again. Toward the book's close, his characters and his readers are left heaving and raw, searching for light along the dark path.

In *Black Coffee*, Ford shows growth not just as a writer, but also as a crafter of multi-faceted beings whose psyches and motives wrestle away from his grasp. Once freed, his characters inflict their own cruelty upon their world. Even so, they often spite themselves just as often as their fellow fictional beings. *Black Coffee*'s men and women have no need for dramatic treatment. They are capable of weaving their own paths of misery, self-inflicted wounds, self-medication, and redemption.

In the work's second story, "343," the reader finds an idyllic Ford character, drowning in equal parts despair, coffee, and booze. Mike, the story's main character, suffers from the death of his wife and an all-but-crippling bout of PTSD. Mike's nonchalance toward his own struggle creates a unique brand of self-torture: a man resigned to his fate of pain and loss. Yet, Mike manages to carve out a modicum of peace in Ford's universe. Similarly, in "Cheap," a trio of characters languish in an inadvertent love triangle in a Manhattan dive bar. Once he is finished setting the scene, Ford allows his characters to breathe and add context to their desperation, crafting a layer of motive and self-determination to their actions in the story's close. Ford's creations tear at their own flesh and then dump a salt shaker onto the sinew, keeping the reader cringing and the pages turning.

But quiet love is also sown into the lining of *Black Coffee*. Before the collection's pain and self-abuse reaches numbing proportions, Ford deftly maneuvers through small, important flashes of love and happiness that shine brighter than some of the stories' moments of languishing emotional defeats. In the titular story, "Black Coffee," Ford draws on personal hardships to polish serene moments of raw affection between a nephew whose life is in transition and an aunt cherishing her final days. "Go Maire Sibh Bhur Saol Nua" encapsulates brief joy in an encounter between an elderly Irish woman with a zest for life and a newly engaged couple on a busy Dublin train. These stories feel especially endearing set against the book's tragedies.

In *Black Coffee*, Ford definitively establishes himself as a writer capable of not only conjuring the darkest parts of the human experience, but also piercing that void like a solitary flame in the night, lighting the path just far enough to keep hope alive.

Dave Pezza

Host of NovelClass

April 8, 2019

14 DANIEL FORD

Branchhall

1.

By the time Tiffany unlocked Branchhall's artificially distressed door, August had been at the bar for an hour.

His notebook open, blank. Nursing a Bloody Mary, the celery wilting from neglect and urban summer. The remains of his third coffee staining the bottom of the white mug. Hangover leaking slowly out of the long feathers tattooed on each of his forearms.

Hank, the head waiter—*maybe the best in town*, August thought—hovered near Tiffany at the hostess stand. He'd been playing the effeminate, judgy Manhattanite with August at the bar. He had the look down—flannel, tight, dark, high-waisted jeans, a waistline Twiggy would blush at thanks to one juice cleanse too many—but Hank didn't have the discipline to hide his Bell Boulevard roots completely.

The coffeemaker behind the bar gurgled and deposited a last gasp of liquid into a clear pot with a dark brown handle. Hank and Tiffany were bracing for duty, their hushed gossip masked by Queens' early afternoon sidewalk chatter and congestion.

"I can't believe I had to give up my brunch plans for this shit," Hank said, eyeing August. "This is next-level sad."

"Straight men get over things slower, you know that," Tiffany said. "You volunteered to switch to this shift, by the way. And don't play like you weren't hung up on Darryl or Ross or whoever that shrimpy barback was a couple weeks back."

"Gross. How dare you. That fucker was get-me-the-hell-out-of-this-city bad news."

"The fuck you gonna go, Queens boy?"

"Places," Hank said. "You follow me on Insta. You know what my dreams are."

"I never check Insta. More of a Snapchat girl," Tiffany said. "I don't need shitheads scrolling back through my feed. One of us should open up the door like Ruby likes."

Hank pushed himself off the podium and sluggishly propped open the door. He stood for a moment outside, looking both ways down the sidewalk.

"Ugh, what's the point?" he asked, watching a couple continue on their way after barely scanning the menu posted outside. "No one is going to set foot in here for hours. If ever."

August raised his hand.

"I'm here," he said, clinking his cup with his knife.

"Don't we know that," Tiffany muttered. "Ruby should be out in a minute."

August hadn't spent a lot of time in the Bronx, but Tiffany made him want to change that. Her long black dreadlocks were both a warning and an invitation. August had gotten as far as threatening a kiss once. She had laughed sweetly before introducing him to her girlfriend.

"I know how she operates," August said. "She'll be down when I reach bottom."

"Bottom of what?" Hank asked.

"If that voice is who I think it is," a voice said from the kitchen, "he doesn't know a bottom. So, he's going to be waiting awhile."

"I don't know why she puts up with you," Hank said. "You don't even pay."

August shrugged and knocked over his Bloody Mary. The red liquid poured out onto the bar and dripped off the edge.

"Oops," he said. "Get your rag out, Bell Blvd."

"You're a fucking asshole," Hank said, already cleaning up the spill. He ran a tight ship, nothing could be out of place or unclean for long, no matter the cause.

"A. Gust., you've got to stop harassing my staff," Ruby said, finally entering the room. "One day I'm not going to be here, and one of them is going to cut your sad sack ass up."

August knew Ruby had been going over menus with her head chef Toby for more than an hour, hectoring him around the ovens. Yet there wasn't a stain or pulled thread anywhere on her tailored black suit. Her matching black heels were an inch too high on purpose and her curly hair was plastered to the sides of her head and tied in an imperial bun. Ruby hit August on the arm with her leather portfolio and knocked his notebook to the floor.

"That thing isn't doing anyone any good, leave it," she said to August. "Hank, throw that out. We get enough trash in here."

Hank swabbed up the notebook in his dirty rag, walked outside, and dumped the notebook into the green city trash can.

"You don't sound surprised that I'm here," August said, more thankful than hurt his nonexistent words were no longer haunting him.

"You are exactly where I thought you'd be today," Ruby said. "Even if we weren't like blood, hurt men are so damn predictable. Only one worse was your father. I knew you'd catch what he's got when you'd cling to his side back there in that kitchen. Figured you'd shake it when he ran off, but look at you. Jeans taken right out of the laundry pile, concert T-shirt, who is that, heh, Foo Fighters, yeah, this is the brokenhearted male's uniform for sure. If this was winter, you'd have on dingy corduroy pants that could start a fire with your thighs. Come have breakfast with me."

Ruby sat down at a table by the window, unworried about taking one of the best seats in the house from a paying customer. She set up shop wherever she wanted and damned the consequences. She gracefully unfolded her napkin and laid it across her lap. Toby appeared at the table at that exact moment, holding a plate of fresh fruit and a cup of yogurt.

"Do you have that honey I like in my yogurt?" Ruby asked, already knowing the answer. Toby grunted something and retreated back into the kitchen.

"He's going to make me wait for that. See what I mean about predictable?" she said to August. "Speaking of, have you talked to her recently?"

August stared down into his coffee cup as he slid into the chair across from Ruby.

"Look at me when I'm talking to you. Hold up your end of the conversation or get your bullshit out of my restaurant."

August shook his head. Then shrugged. He ran his hand through his shaggy brown hair and raised his eyes just enough.

"A birthday message. A butt dial," he said. "A song lyric here and there. That tends to happen whenever I think about her. It just pops up. Like a reminder that ..."

Ruby coughed into her hand and pointed toward the door.

"What do you want from me?" August asked.

"I want you to acknowledge you think about her all the time. In fact, say her name. Eleanor. Women like it when they're referred to by their names."

"Ruby, for chrissakes, I just wanted to nurse my hangover."

"You wanted a willing shoulder and some easy platitudes. You know that's not me. Tough love and coffee, kid, you knew that when you walked in the door. I've known you two as a couple since you swayed on in here drunk on cheap-ass wine, I'm guessing, pawing at each other at my bar. You stole lemons and limes and strawberries to make that girl laugh. Who do you think got you drunker? Gave you that courage to think you weren't going to fuck it all up from the jump. I've got two restaurants to run. Working on expanding to a third, in Brooklyn of all places. I've got limited time to fill this particular black stereotype. And the only reason I'm doing it at all is ... ?"

"What?"

"You know."

"We're family."

"Such as it is, yes."

Ruby had known August his whole life. She watched him grow from a quiet, stoic kid with no family to a man with pretty good sense and prospects when he wasn't moping on a barstool. She'd gotten farther in her life than her family ever expected, and had further to go, but she couldn't quite shake her connection to August. Her friends teased her while devouring whatever gossip she had, calling her a "black fairy godmother" or worse. She shouldn't be so invested—she had actual investments to worry about—but while she hadn't had a choice in this family, it was what she had left too.

"Mutual friend of ours is getting married," August finally said. "First time we'll be seeing each other since, you know."

"Jesus, I'm surprised you're not still drunk."

"I think I am a little."

"Either of you in the wedding party?"

"Just me."

"Let's take a moment to celebrate that fact, shall we?" Ruby said, lifting her mimosa and taking a deep swallow. "Don't ruin some poor girl's wedding. Although that would give you something to write about. How's that going? You got another movie in that trashed notebook or what?"

"Or what," August said. "I think I jotted down a recipe in there. Hey, I wrote one, didn't I?"

"Oh, did that set you up for life?" Ruby asked. "Can I expect you to get straight with your tab?"

"Working on it. This isn't helping. She's not helping."

"You didn't write with her either."

"Yeah, but I thought about writing."

"Well, that'll sure make you flush. Let's start with what you want to happen."

"I want to scream at her in the parking lot. Right when she gets out of her car."

"You worried she might be with someone?"

"Shit, I am now."

"Think she got a plus-one?"

August crossed his arms over his chest.

"I think someone would have told me," he said. "If she did, I might not be invited. Or someone's sick enough to want me to sabotage the wedding."

"But you don't think any of that's true."

"No, let's assume she's single and I'm letting her have it."

"Go on then," Ruby said.

"I could put my ending on this. I stood there like a jackass and took it from her last time. Tried to just cut her deep out of my life. Look how well that's gone. Anyway, we all know how the story of the poor boy fighting the rich family ends. I'll just shove cake into my mouth and go home and drink myself blind."

"Well, just in case you do go in guns blazing, and I do mean that figuratively, because lord knows this country has lost its damn mind, we don't need me on TV talking and lying about how I didn't see this shit coming," Ruby said. "Why don't you riff on me first. What are you going to say if she's standing right in front of you and you've got your filter off?"

"I'm not really feeling up—"

"Not gonna ask again."

August pressed his fingertip between his eyebrows, closed his eyes, and said, "I know the last time we talked I sat there awkwardly and stayed silent and weird like I promised I wouldn't. Maybe it wouldn't have changed anything if I had been like this. But I'm going to talk now and you're going to listen. I want to get the good shit out of the way first.

"I hated saying 'I love you.' I always felt like it undersold what we had, what I felt about you. How I wanted you to feel about yourself. Whatever my feelings were for you. Whatever those emotions were. Or bond. Or connection. Whatever it was. 'Love' was, and is, such a pedestrian word for all of it. An understatement. Less than you deserved.

"Every day I found something, or multiple somethings, that made me fall in love with you more. I woke up smiling, thinking—well, knowing really—that each new revelation was just around the corner.

"And you ended it all. When it was just starting to get to the tough part. When everything got real and scary and complicated. When our lives were going to change no matter what we did. And you couldn't pick the path that would have given you some of the happiness you've craved your whole life.

"You gave us no good options. We could have planned together. Good or bad, we could have talked it out. God damn, that's all we did all the time. And now we're here. Whatever time we get out here and that's it."

"Oh, is that all?" Ruby said.

"Fuck, Ruby, I just want to scream at her until my voice breaks. And then I can walk free. Freer at least."

"Hmm," she said, throwing her napkin down.

"What? No good?"

"You don't need me," she said. "I was right, you're a waste of my time. Finish the omelet I've got coming for you and then get the hell out."

"Pleasure as always," August mumbled.

Ruby leaned back in her seat, pissed as hell at what she was about to do for family.

2.

Eleanor hunted for the lone cigarette she had jailed in a pack buried at the bottom of her purse. She sat in a snug corner of an urban park surrounded by stubby brick apartment buildings. She re-crossed her legs, feeling her skin unpeel—slick with late summer sweat. The willow tree under which she broke up with August scratched at her back.

She didn't smoke—hated it, in fact—but knew that there would be a moment—*this* moment—that forced her to indulge in the habit that eventually killed her father.

"He'd be so proud," she muttered, wondering if he'd be more impressed by all the beautiful ways she had fucked up her life. She had inherited his stringy strawberry blond hair, which she always wore up, always, and fiery temper, so why not his genius for self-destruction?

She dug past lip balm, old concert ticket stubs, napkins, plastic forks, fistfuls of scrunched up cash, a bag of old oyster crackers her grandmother had given her. A bright red lipstick she reserved for no one these days. Plenty of detritus from August's love. Reminders she didn't need but couldn't part with. She gave up looking for that pack of smokes that likely had been given away long ago. She could feel the defiant bristle of the rural wilderness within her as she squeezed a tarnished tab from a can of American beer in her palm.

Eleanor grew up in a dive bar.

She knew August never understood that. How her family built itself up from second-hand neon and only Busch on tap. How her mother studied from two a.m. to six a.m. to get her law degree, while going to class whenever she could skip a shift. How she founded a practice helping drunks most likely to show up at the bar and spend the legal fees she was owed on cigarettes out of the vending machine. How the murder of twin girls broke her heart and then padded their bank account when she became a household name defending their killer. How she cast out her deadbeat husband but still paid his expenses because she couldn't let anyone—or anything—suffer, even if they inflicted that suffering back on her.

Their life was nothing, and she made her money on nothing people. She gave it freely to them so they could be something people. Eleanor didn't feel entitled, and she knew August tried not to see her that way. But his life had been so much harder. She had eventually broken out of her mother's professional shadow by choosing nonprofit work, but how could he not think of her life as anything but charmed. In truth, all she really needed was him. He just always seemed to fight to give her more, much more than his spirit or wallet could handle.

Which, of course, is why she had to rip his heart out.

"Look who it is," a familiar voice said.

Eleanor checked the time on her cell phone.

"You run a restaurant, how is it possible you're here right now," she asked.

"Brunch bores me," Ruby said. "I employ other people to care about it for me."

"And you just happen to run into me."

"My weekly routine. I contemplate life here."

"What do you have in the basket?" Eleanor asked, smoothing out her navy skirt that had robins soaring through the creases. "You've got cheese and wine in there, don't you?"

"A selection of brie, gouda, and Havarti with dill," Ruby said. "Half-carafe of a Malbec I'm in love with. The best bacon, lettuce, tomato sandwiches you've ever had."

"Again, just your normal routine, right?"

"I treat myself *very* well."

The two women ate in silence, watching the rowing crews slice through the river.

"Have you talked to him?" Eleanor finally asked.

"Only reason I'm here right now," Ruby said. "Got my own problems, but I'm here talking to another person I'm fond of about shit they don't really need help with. You'll know the things you'll do for family if you don't already."

"Yeah, well," Eleanor said. "He must have had a few choice words for me."

"That boy barely has words to fill a thimble. Especially when he's hurt."

"There was so much screaming at the end, Ruby. All from me. He never raised his voice to me. He'd be annoyed at me, sure, and we'd fight, all the time about everything, but it was like fencing to him. Succinct movements and counterattacks. I could be so awful to him and he'd just parry and dance me into the next conversation. Except that day. I had to be a battering ram."

"You had to overdo it to make it feel like it was your decision. Not your mother's."

"So, you knew?"

"I know who that ... woman is. That's all the information I need."

"Pretty sure I convinced myself it was real by the time I walked away. Oh yeah, I had to turn my back to him. He couldn't even give me that. Bastard. Just stood there, stoic, looking at, whatever the fuck. I expected all these texts and emails, but there was nothing. I couldn't even stalk him on social media. I watched him block me from every channel in succession. Felt like a casket being snapped closed."

"I never should have encouraged you two," Ruby said. "It was always going to end this way."

"And I'm an independent woman, let's be clear about that," Eleanor said. "I don't need him or anyone else. It's just one love. I can win another like that."

"Not if it was the right love, to begin with," Ruby said. "You want what you want. There's girl power, or whatever the fuck they call it now, in that. We can have both. Men and power. We don't need to pick."

"I'm just ... infected." Eleanor said. "Infected by him. Infected by that abandoned love."

"Well, you're both dramatic as hell," Ruby said. "I'll give you that."

A pair of joggers ran by, their ponytails swishing happily, their feet and legs in perfect rhythm. Eleanor stood up and walked over to the paved running path. She stretched her arms out and then put her hands on her hips. Ruby put down her sandwich, flicked the crumbs off her dress, and walked over.

"The love started here and ended here, huh?" Ruby asked.

Eleanor nodded. She pressed her finger against one of her eyes, trying to stop the tears from leaking out.

"You know him," Eleanor said. "Everything is a scene. I made him fight for every inch from before the first date to the last. He had a perfect picnic. I'm guessing some of that might have been your handiwork. I steeled myself against any wonderfulness he could possibly think up. He was just so earnest. Less than a dime to his name, which I only assumed at the time. I didn't know for sure until later. Knowing who I was, where I came from. He didn't care about any of that. He just wanted to be with me. Even if it was just for a meal. Or coffee. Or one too many drinks at a dive bar."

"Oh yeah, we've established you're not emotional at all," Ruby said, swatting Eleanor's sleeve. "What was it he said?"

"What?"

"To make you put your guard down?"

"I don't remember, to be honest with you."

"Girl, this would be a lot easier ..."

"Fine," Eleanor said, stomping back to her blanket. "I was bragging about my mother. I know how you feel about her, but she's earned everything she has. She had just won some big case or something. I was really proud. And I knew all the details the press didn't know. I was showing off. And I couldn't stop talking because he was making me nervous just by wanting me so much."

"And he said ..."

Eleanor grimaced.

"Maybe you're special too," she said. "He then forced me to talk about myself. And I told him everything. I couldn't stop. I didn't stop. I'm still talking to him in my head. That's why I was the one who eventually broke down and texted him. Emailed him all those song lyrics. What a monster I am."

"Is that really how you feel, woman?" Ruby asked. "Also, people infected with shit don't spend this long worrying over it. They just knife it out."

"No," Eleanor said. "I feel lucky. That I had it at all. And have whatever's left."

"That's what I thought," Ruby said, collecting their trash, throwing it into the basket. "I'd pay good money to see what goes down at this wedding, but god knows you two will find your way to telling me."

"Or we make the news."

"Don't think I won't have my TV tuned to CNN just in case," Ruby said. "Don't go soft on each other. Ain't got time to leave something unburied."

"That what you told him?" Eleanor asked.

"I didn't have to," Ruby said, getting up to walk away. "You're going to get an earful if he doesn't wuss out. I'd listen."

3.

August forked a pile of wedding cake into his mouth and immediately spit it back out. The path of cherry goo that split the piece down the middle tasted like gummy chemicals. He tossed his utensil toward the middle of the empty table and listened to it clang against the copper-wrought centerpiece.

"Coffee? Tea?" a waiter asked him.

"Coffee, please," August said. "Pour two if you could. I'm going to need back up. These bores aren't coming back. They won't mind if I borrow a mug."

"Ha," the waiter said. "Very good, sir."

August watched the thinning crowd on the dance floor as he raised his cup to his nose. The coffee smelled like it tasted—awful, but it was hot and black. There were worse things in the world than bad, free coffee.

He couldn't help but be impressed by the remaining dancers. Fueled by watered-down gin and tonics and light, rice-based beer (*from a cash bar,* thought August, *the humanity*), and food burnt to its last earthen flavors so as not to offend any allergies or culinary expectations, these red-faced, gyrating, grinding, and, yes, happy guests were doing their best to suck out the final embers of enjoyment from a party sorely lacking in it. The clichéd music barely dulled their senses. Could-be lovers rocked into each other, longtime husbands twirled their disaffected and privileged wives, and awkward teenagers (some of whom looked like they had been sampling half-empty drinks all night) risked acne and social suicide to thrust their hips to benign rock 'n' roll.

August hated them all for how jealous they made him. He woke up that morning determined that he wasn't going to feel anything at this point in the evening. He'd either be too drunk or too deep in conversation with an interested female to have to choke down this kind of emotional carnage. He'd gone to bury her ghost at Branchhall, what more did the universe want?

He knew answers to any of the questions he could have asked her would never come. He could never tell if he was at the beginning of something with her or at the end, but, now, fighting the urge to weep into an inedible wedding cake, surely felt like the end.

"Can I just say something?" Eleanor asked.

"Gah!" August said, his whole body twitching in surprise. "How do you do this every time? Can't a guy just enjoy his coffee?"

"It started out as accidental but then became sport."

"Well, bully for you. You don't have to say anything."

"You've done a good job of avoiding me all night. You can go back to it when I leave. Can you just let—"

"I get it. I understand. Don't worry about it."

"You don't even know—"

"Oh, I know. Don't worry about it."

"Listen, interrupt one more time, I'm going to—"

"There's nothing you can do or say that I'm not already doing or saying to myself. That doesn't make any sense, but you get it. Nothing more needs to be said. I get it. I understand."

"Is that why—"

"I'm not crying!"

"I wasn't going to say you were crying!"

"Oh, well."

"Okay, can I talk? I've been thinking about what to say and I need to say it. Even though I've done all the real talking up to this point in our relationship."

"Sorry. Yeah. I get it," August said, preparing to listen.

"Don't start already with the nodding and the face," Eleanor said. "Your stupid face. That face."

"I'm not doing anything with my face," he said, clenching his jaw.

"Then point it at me and shut up."

August knew the tears were flowing out of his left eye, the one furthest away from her. As soon as he turned his head, she was going to know. He didn't mind her knowing he was sad, but he felt awful that she was going to torture herself over the fact he was sad because of her.

"You're always trying to protect me," Eleanor said. "Just meet me eye-to-eye this one time."

"Stop reading my—"

Eleanor put both hands on August's cheeks and turned his head. She wiped the tears away, even though they kept coming. More so now that he felt her skin on his, maybe for the last time.

She sat back for a moment, one hand still on his cheek, shaking. Maybe he was shaking. He couldn't tell the difference. There was no preparing for what came next. He'd just have to let it run over him. He knew it was likely to stay stuck in there, rather than pass through a clean exit wound.

Eleanor moved one hand down to his chest. She held it there as the music stopped and guests moved off the dance floor to collect their jackets, purses, and long-abandoned high heels. The full ballroom lights snapped on. Groans were heard as people took in the full damage that had been hidden by mood lighting and cocktails.

"Are you going to say anything?" August mumbled. "I could stay like this all night, but at some point, my heart will explode. And then I'll get hungry. Cranky. I could use a nap. Been a long day."

Eleanor moved her hand over his mouth. She smiled and said, "Maybe you're special too."

4.

Branchhall's evening staff had been dismissed, the door bolted. Ruby's table by the window was littered with spreadsheets and vendor invoices, some splashed with dark maroon drops from her three-quarters empty bottle of Malbec.

Ruby dumped the last quarter into her oversized glass and tossed a thick envelope back into the mail pile. She sat back, stretched her arms above her head. She resolved to head home when she saw a figure step out of a gypsy cab and stride right for the door and knock hard three times. Ruby downed most of what was left of the wine and calmly walked to the front.

"A. Gust.," Ruby said, opening the door. "Right on time."

August smirked and looked back out toward the car.

"Good work," Ruby said. "Grab two stools at the bar. No stealing shit this time and no freebies. Make her pay, it'll build character."

Eleanor bounced in the door, walked past August, and hugged Ruby tightly, whispering something in her ear. Ruby smiled, took a breath, and then started laughing. Eleanor offered August her arm.

"Since I put us so far behind, I'll lead the way, darling."

August and Eleanor sat down in front of two waiting cocktail glasses.

"Well," Ruby said. "Let us begin again, shall we?"

1.

A stuffed duck peered at Mike from a shelf above the cashier's head.

Ducks were her favorite. He didn't remember why. She was just crazy about them. She made him call her *baby duck*. It was the only pet name they had, and she always lit up when he said it.

"Sir?"

"Yes, ma'am?"

"Your change?"

The teenage cashier with too many piercings and tattoos awkwardly held three bucks and a handful of coins in front of him. She was more annoyed than confused. There was a line— the usual suburban snake of grumps, foot-tappers, and thrifts eager to use their coupons.

"Right."

"Do you want a receipt?"

"No, that's okay."

As Mike started walking away, someone pulled his jacket.

"Excuse me? You forgot your bag."

The woman had blond hair and heels.

"Thanks. Lost in my thoughts. I appreciate it."

"Any time," she said. "You mind me asking if you were over there?"

She motioned to the dog tags on his key chain.

"Yes, ma'am."

"In that case, I should be thanking *you*."

"That's not necessary. I was doing it for my mother."

"A momma's boy, huh?"

"Born and raised."

"And here I thought you guys were just bags of muscles."

"I've got those too, but I love my momma."

She giggled. Her laugh sounded like Muddy Waters' "Kansas City" on vinyl.

Mike felt a pinch in the back of his neck.

"What are the odds you let a grateful citizen buy you a drink?" she asked.

"It's a little early."

"Didn't say it had to be alcoholic," she said.

"'A waste of a drinking occasion,' my father would have said."

"Come on, we can start with coffee."

Mix caffeine with whatever was happening? Mike thought. *Probably not a good idea.*

He was attracted to her honey maple rasp and stonewashed eyes, but he could feel the sweat moving in a long stream down the back of his knee. His socks were drenched inside his boots.

"Rain check."

Mike's father didn't raise him to avoid giving his name and number to a beautiful woman, but he needed to immediately freak out in a secure bivouac. Outside, fall was closer than it had been yesterday. He tossed his bag in the trash and marched to his car, not even remembering what he bought.

Deep breaths, he thought.

Mike was still sweating when he sat down in the driver's seat, but he wasn't as angry. He started the car and turned the radio on. Music helped him ease out of it. He popped open the glove compartment. A picture of her was taped inside.

"Home," he said.

The GPS charted his route. He turned his blinker on and waited for the traffic to die down so he could make a left turn. It took a bit, but the delay made him feel less surly.

"Fuckin' duck."

2.

"Are we ever going to leave this bed?"

"God, I hope not."

"We have to at least attempt to do something today."

"I'd argue that we've done plenty already."

"I mean real things."

"That all seemed pretty real to me. Seriously, what could you possibly want to do out there when you could keep making love to me in here?"

"You're insatiable. Aren't you hungry? I'm hungry."

"One of us can go get food and the other could stay here and hold down the love fort."

"Don't say 'love fort' ever again."

"Roger that."

"Trying to get used to the lingo already? Can you believe the draft went that high?"

"With our luck, yes."

"The news says things are improving, but now we need more muscle over there?"

"I'll give you a full briefing when I get back."

"I prefer you give it to me right now."

"Yes, ma'am."

"Ugh. 'Ma'am' doesn't sound good on me."

"Everything sounds good on you."

"He bedded the girl and is still in hot pursuit. You're not going to use those lines on other women over there are you?"

"Come on, give me some credit. I'd never reuse old material."

"Bastard."

"We're not going anywhere, so get back under the covers."

"Fine, but only because I'm chilly."

"Pretty sure all my heat is gravitating to one place at the moment."

"Well, I'll just have to go where the heat is, I guess. Consider this your incentive to come home."

"Yes, ma'am."

"Now I'm using teeth."

3.

Mike's fifth therapy session didn't go well.

He didn't mind talking about things, which made his panic attacks even more arbitrary. If he were anyone else, every session would feature a breakthrough. For him, it was chatting with a therapist who seemed just as disappointed that they hadn't found anything close to a root cause.

Damn my parents for being loving and supportive, Mike thought. *Would have been easy to pin all this on an abusive mother or absent father.*

"Are the attacks happening more or less frequently?" Ernest asked.

"Same amount. More powerful."

"Takes time."

"I've been back a while."

This room reminded Mike of most of the accommodations over there—federally mandated gray walls and IKEA-like furniture built by the lowest bidder. Ernest didn't have a beard, which unnerved him a little bit. The guy could probably go a month or two without shaving.

How much knowledge and life experience could he actually have without the ability to grow facial hair? Mike thought.

Ernest paused his questioning to write a few more illegible lines in his notebook. He did a lot of writing during these sessions, which also caused Mike anxiety. His pen movements were swift, especially when he was crossing out full paragraphs. Mike was impressed that someone could think out loud and on the page simultaneously—even if that person was wrong most of the time.

"Do you feel like killing anyone during these episodes?"

"No. Feels more like high school heartbreak."

"Did someone break your heart in high school?"

"Of course. Feels like we're fishing here."

"We are. Could you possibly have anything else to reveal?"

"I was an altar boy as a kid."

"Did you get molested?"

"No."

"Too bad. You'd be rich."

Mike had told him about the killing. The fear, the sweating, the loneliness, the firefights, the bullets he took, the blood, her death, the crying. The ability to open up about it all only provided more questions.

Ernest rubbed his cheek where his therapist beard should have been.

"Can you still get it up?" he asked.

"You're pretty old. Can you get it up?"

"Nothing wrong with your sense of humor. So you didn't think of any fresh ideas?"

"It's pretty random."

"Like the duck?"

"Like the duck."

"Thinking about her doesn't necessarily trigger an episode then?"

"If it did, I'd be in an asylum by now."

"You think about the good and the bad?"

"Everything. I cry about it. I have a drink. I usually don't have to flee the premises or check myself into the emergency room."

"You don't remember going?"

"Not until I regained consciousness. Woke up to a pretty hot nurse. Wish I hadn't soiled myself when I walked in."

"What were you doing before?"

"Can't remember. In line for a movie maybe? I vaguely remember a woman screaming into a phone."

"How many of your buddies died over there?"

"We lost guys too fast. I didn't have time to make friends. I can't picture faces. I only have snippets of a couple of guys. How he was shot. What info was on his dog tags. A hometown or two."

"Ever feel guilty you survived?"

More old territory, Mike thought. *Spinning in circles.*

"Yeah, but I've always had bad luck. I guess I was saving up all my good luck to make it back. Living and carrying on seemed the best way to honor those guys who didn't make it. Certainly better than being angry all the time."

"Damn."

"What?"

"You're well-adjusted."

"I know. Pisses me off, too."

4.

Mike examined a bright blue beer bottle before bringing it to his lips.

Bud Light sucks unless you're drinking it for free on a back deck with your brother, he thought.

He was alone at the moment. Phil had gone in search of meat they could dump on the grill. God willing, he'd return with a pair of cigars as well.

Phil and Mike didn't have to be soldiers here. Phil had served well before all the real shit went down, but the system had used him just the same. Wounds of peace could be just as deep as those from war.

"Burgers?" Phil asked from the screen door.

"Got hot dogs?"

"Both?"

"Affirmative."

Mike finished his beer and started another.

"How's therapy?" Phil asked, carrying a plate of red beef patties and pale hot dogs.

"Fine. You?"

"I'm still fucked up."

"I'm not. It's a problem."

"Want to fucking switch, Sally?"

"Just stating a fact."

"Seriously, let's trade my aggression and depression for your 'episodes.' Jesus, you fought a war for years. I get a decade's worth of paper cuts and I can't sleep at night. Shit's fucked up, man."

"You did more than that," Mike said.

He let his brother rant for a while and then got up to examine the disaster on the grill.

"These animals are deader than they were the first time," Mike said.

"Shut the fuck up."

"What are we going to eat now?"

"Adjust your skirt, sit down, and finish your fucking beer."

Phil scooped up the blackened meat and dumped it into the trash barrel.

"You want help?" Mike asked.

"I'm not going to fucking tell you again. Keep fucking drinking!"

Mike laughed as Phil went back into the house fuming and did as he was told. He pounded his beer and then guzzled the next one. Then he opened up another and eased back into his deck chair.

While Phil dealt with solving their dinner crisis, Mike stretched out his legs. The alcohol was starting to hit home. His boots felt heavy and reassuring on his feet. Someone suggested he give sneakers a try, but Mike knew he'd never feel safe. Boots kept him ready. Poised.

He woke up one morning to find mortar shells for breakfast. The forward operating base's makeshift walls fell apart like particle board. His roommate grabbed his M16, headed into the heat without his boots, slipped on the recently waxed tile in the hallway, and was decapitated by a shoulder-fired missile. Mike put his boots on, threw the body over his shoulder, and grabbed the head by the hair. A wall collapsed on him soon after. A military working dog found him a day later alongside the pieces of his roommate. He was half dead, but still had his boots—the only things he needed to stay alive.

"Chinese will be here in thirty minutes," Phil said, returning bare-chested. What was left of his shirt ended up with the discarded meat. He slammed the grill cover and roughly threw on a white V-neck T-shirt. Mike would check his brother's walls for holes later.

"You didn't even ask what I wanted."

"You haven't ordered anything other than chicken and broccoli since you've been alive."

"Maybe I wanted to switch it up."

"I just calmed down," Phil said. "Do you think you could lay off?"

He couldn't have been too mad because he revealed a pair of Ashton cigars. Mike pressed the dark brown tobacco under his nose and inhaled deeply.

There isn't a flower or perfume that smells this good, Mike thought.

Phil lit his and walked to the far corner of the deck, becoming a small burnt orange smudge. His midsection was fuller now, but his arms still contained the brawn he developed during his military career. Both brothers had inherited their mother's obsidian hair, but Phil's was graying prematurely, like their father's. Phil smoked his cigar like he did most things: swiftly and without enjoyment. He put it out in the half-broken terracotta platter next to him long before Mike reached the midway point of his.

"You're an asshole," Phil said.

"But a concerned one. You're lucky to have me as a brother."

The brothers waited for the food on the deck despite a temperature drop.

"You remember when Mom would force Dad to grill during the winter?" Phil asked after what felt like a year of silence.

"I don't think anyone ever forced Dad to do anything. I think it was the other way around. Dad forced his grilling on Mom."

Their father loved being in charge of dinner. He'd grill anything and everything. Mike remembered him stationed in the backyard wearing a Yankees beanie. Half-frozen beer on the side burner he never used. The dog whined incessantly to be let out, but their mother wouldn't dare because that mutt would have died lying out there in the snow waiting for the old man. His face used to get redder than the raw meat. Mike couldn't remember him happier.

Their father never talked as much as when he was out there with a poker or spatula in his hand. He wouldn't shut up. If he had to have a serious discussion with anyone, he'd bring home a couple pounds of steak tips and take forever to cook them. Whoever needed straightening out would be standing out there in all kinds of weather willing the fire to burn hotter so they could run into the house where he wasn't chewing their asses out. The family had the mother of all cookouts when he died.

He never saw Mike in uniform.

"What was that bird he tried to cook once? You know, the one where Mom ended up so pissed because it tasted like gravel?" Phil asked.

"Pheasant?"

"That's it. Worst Thanksgiving ever."

"Pretty sure we ended up at McDonald's and you threw up after eating twenty chicken nuggets in five minutes."

Mike's stomach burped, reminding him their takeout was late. He could tell Phil was anxious because he kept lighting his shoelace on fire and then quickly extinguishing it. He didn't stop until the material blackened and fell into a pile of ash below his feet. The metallic scratch of the lighter held Mike's attention until he started drooling boorishly. Phil smacked his arm in the "what the fuck's wrong with you" manner only brothers can pull off right.

"You're sure you're not messed up?"

"Yep," Mike said. "I'm going to take a piss."

"Breaking the seal two beers in. That does not bode well for the rest of this evening."

"I've had seven."

"In that case, make sure you don't piss all over my floor. Find some toilet water!"

Phil's bathroom was still his wife's. She had moved in with her mother when Phil had gotten too aggressive to be around her and the boy. They spoke often. She wasn't giving up on him. They made it work and the kid was handling it well. They were functionally maladjusted.

The beer flowed swiftly out of Mike. His head felt a little fuzzy, but he wasn't drunk. He couldn't remember the last time he drank enough to feel inebriated. The medication kept him pretty level.

Mike glanced at the clock on the wall. It was stopped at a quarter to four. He had no idea how long he'd been here. He hadn't wanted to stay this late. It had been days since he last visited her. He dried his hands on the pink hand towel and headed back toward the deck.

Phil had lit all the faux bamboo torches surrounding the deck. A half dozen takeout cartons were on the kitchen table.

Mike didn't feel hungry, he felt panicked. Maybe he was drunk.

Drank and smoked too much without eating, he thought. *As always.*

However, his body told him he wasn't cocked. He couldn't tell if he was dizzy or disoriented from the water now pouring out of his eyes. He knocked over a food container trying to grab onto a chair. Phil yelled from outside. Something about being careful.

His legs gave way, but his boots kept him upright. Mike took another deep breath and tried to focus his attention on the screen door. If he could get there, Phil would realize he needed help.

The deck was on fire. Mike blinked a few times to prove what he was seeing was real. Phil hadn't been annoyed; he was the one in danger.

Mike's training took over. He burst through the screen door, leaving it hanging stunned on its hinges. He wrapped his arms around Phil's midsection and sent them both into the calm surface of the pool.

The spiky smell of chlorine invaded Mike's nostrils and he lost consciousness before he could realize the fire hadn't been real.

5.

Mike finally made it to the cemetery after he left the hospital.

Phil had been in the bed next to him with a few broken ribs. There was a bouquet of flowers on the table near his bed. Mike was discharged before his brother woke up, but he was pretty sure Phil had been faking sleep so he didn't have to talk to him.

Mike noticed someone had brought her flowers as well. They looked out of place though. She never cared much for plants. She preferred to have a bowl of fruit or a painting to add color to a room. Something she couldn't kill and then feel guilty about.

Mike had been sweating through his fatigues in a desert mess hall when she died.

A full bird colonel had approached him on his way back to his bunk. He hadn't had his helmet on during morning drills, so he had braced himself for a good hiding. Half the world was on fire, but God forbid his lid was unprotected. Protocol trumps perspective in the Army.

He had given Mike the news empathetically. He had saluted the officer, thanked him, and went to his bunk to cry privately. Nothing happened at first, but eventually, he wept for days.

The enemy had sent snipers to the United States. It took a while to eliminate them all. The Army had to take over a few cities. There were refugees at Denny's and Costco. Traitors were suspected everywhere. The news media would have gone even crazier had the government not suspended the First Amendment for a few months. It took years to sort out. All the soldiers defending their home turf ended up institutionalized. Forgotten.

She ended up in the ground.

There was no romance to it. She hadn't been driving to meet Mike's incoming flight. She just ran into dumb luck with a bullet attached to it. Copycat snipers sprang up in a few towns. She had been stopped at a red light, the bullet pierced the windshield. Mike had heard from some people in town that a few assholes behind her had honked their horns.

He never knew what to do standing in front of a tombstone. Typically, he hung around until his feet hurt. He thought about and discussed her so much outside these gates that he had nothing left by the time he visited.

Despite her preference for life and happiness, she was much more comfortable dealing with death than he was. She had an older family, so she dutifully attended funerals, brought holiday decorations to cemeteries, and recited a handful of prayers if nothing else seemed appropriate. She knew when to be solemn and when to lighten the mood. Mike was by her side for quite a few of those moments, and she never failed to make everyone feel a little better. Mike, on the other hand, giggled awkwardly when he should have been silent and stoic. He was assigned grave duty when he first landed over there. He just dug the holes, filling them in was another private's job. He kept death at arm's length, and it rewarded him with a ticket home and a lover in a casket.

At least Mike's episodes abated while he stood here motionless. That's how he knew she didn't have anything to do with what was happening to him. Memories of her, large and small, were everywhere he went, and they were always welcome additions to his daily life. He wasn't religious by any stretch, but he believed there was a script people couldn't possibly understand. It wasn't his time to be with her, so Mike had to be satisfied with the time that came before.

When he got drafted, both of them just assumed they'd have plenty of time to work it out when he returned. *If* he returned. He often thought about what their wedding day would have been like. Her side of the church would have been full. He supposed he could have hired a few people to supplement his shrinking family. All of his friends (and Phil) would be standing up beside him. She probably would have taken pity on him and loaned him a few bodies so that his parents weren't lonely.

Mike would have loved her wholeheartedly forever.

He checked the time discreetly. He didn't want her to think he was bored. After his poolside heroics, the doctors upped his medication. Mike figured they would have been impressed that his subconscious instincts led him to help instead of hurt. Over there, he would have been given a medal and a promotion. The Army may have even burned down the deck to ensure the feel-good story had a ring of truth to it. Instead, Mike got six pills and a schedule.

"Goodbye, baby duck," he said.

Mike couldn't keep a smile from forming on his face. He let it have its moment before he headed to his car.

6.

Mike took an open seat at the counter of his favorite diner.

Diners were one of the rare things they disagreed on. She hated them. She always complained the food was too greasy.

She had a strange phobia of eating where she could watch her food being cooked.

"Coffee?" Thomas, the owner, asked, already pouring Mike a cup.

His gentle face was betrayed by a pair of thick horn-rimmed glasses he claimed he had been wearing since the late 1950s. He opened the place at five a.m. thirty years ago, yet his button-down shirt and black slacks didn't have a visible stain or wrinkle. He was lean, bald, and the horniest widower Mike had ever met.

"Actually, do you have tea?"

"Are you shitting me?"

"Yes, keep pouring."

"I'll be back with your chili, asshole."

Mike didn't make it a habit of pairing chili with his morning coffee. He was skirting the line between breakfast and lunch, so Thomas was probably hedging his bets. He liked to have Mike's food ready before he ordered it. Thomas never gave him a menu and loved to use him as a guinea pig for new recipes. He didn't charge, so Mike couldn't complain about the extra bathroom time some of the man's experiments induced.

Mike added a few extra sugars to eliminate some of his coffee's strength. He listened in on the conversation the older regulars were having about the hometown AAA team's late-inning loss last night. So-and-so blew the save, and the much-heralded, brawny outfielder struck out four times. These old timers were cataloging statistics with the ease of Bill James. They were even sophisticated enough to include WAR, FIP, and OPS+, but most of them agreed that they were bullshit. A guy was a baseball player or he wasn't.

Mike tuned out and absorbed the diner's music. He was convinced Thomas had his daughter positioned in front of a cassette tape boom box. Mike did have to admit that there usually was a respectable blend of oldies, folk, and classic rock. There were few places in the world he was able to relax (thanks to recent events, that list was even smaller), but he felt right at home with these old bastards, degenerates, and hungover hipsters.

"I had a feeling I'd run into you soon enough," a voice said behind him.

Mike swiveled in his seat and found himself staring at a familiar pair of long legs. She had her blond hair worked into a ponytail, which matched perfectly with her dark yoga pants and purple sneakers. Her torso was all rebel; she wore a Nine Inch Nails T-shirt and a black leather jacket that made him long for a Marlboro Red.

"You going to gawk or ask me to join you?" she asked.

The typically mute and motionless South American regular sitting next to Mike immediately shifted to the next open stool as soon as he caught sight of her. He encouraged her to sit down with his broken English and wayward eyes.

"Do you mind?" she asked.

"Of course not, ma'am," Mike said. "But I'd watch him, he gets handsy."

The guy didn't understand but nodded his head vigorously.

"I'll take my chances," she said. "Do all military guys talk like you?"

"We're polite killers. I'm Mike."

"Nikki."

She grabbed his hand before he had a chance to fully extend it. Her grip was as strong as any commanding officer's.

"What can I get you, darling?" Thomas asked.

Mike noticed his baritone dropped an octave.

"Oh, I'll have whatever he's having," she said.

"He's having coffee and chili."

"Really?"

Mike shrugged.

"Well, that won't do," Nikki said. "What do you recommend?"

"For you?" Thomas gave her an exaggerated once over, which made her giggle. "Tea, scone, and half of my bank account after our inevitable divorce."

"Make it a blueberry muffin and you've got a deal. They look delicious!"

"Can I expect my omelet any time soon?" Mike asked.

"You're getting chicken pot pie today. Homemade. You're going to love it," Thomas said. "At least you better, I ordered ingredients for a week."

Thomas walked away, but not before giving Mike a couple of animated fist pumps.

"So, this is where you hang out?" Nikki asked.

"Either here or the strip club," Mike said. "I work the afternoon shift."

"I'd pay good money to see that. What do you actually do for a living?"

Shit, Mike thought.

He wasn't looking for anything, but he certainly didn't want to scare her away completely. Another added bonus of surviving that desert cemetery was a decent combat pension that allowed him to be pretty fluid about employment. He worked as a bouncer one night, a grocery clerk the next. He may have even worked security for a local strip club. The low point was signing up to be a clown at a farm hosting an event for military families. Some kid stole his red nose.

"Well, I ..."

A hand slapped Mike's back. He almost spilled his coffee all over Nikki. Ernest's clean-shaven chin appeared over his shoulder.

Gang's all here, Mike thought.

"This cover band is making a hash of this Warren Zevon song, don't you think?" Ernest asked.

"I think this is him," Mike said. "The speakers suck."

"You guys want to move this to that table that just opened up?" Thomas asked. "I'll send this knucklehead's chili over when you get settled."

"Chili and coffee?" Ernest asked.

"We've been here already," Mike said. "Don't knock it until you've tried it."

Nikki eagerly strutted over to the table. Mike caught Ernest's arm.

"Is this allowed?"

"As long as I pay, sure," Ernest said.

"In that case, after you."

"You mind if I excuse myself to use the ladies' room first?" Nikki asked.

Mike made a big show of gesturing toward the restrooms. His goal was to keep her interested long enough to figure out if he could still be interesting.

"You like Warren Zevon?" Ernest asked.

"He's okay."

"Do you have a favorite song?"

"I'm partial to 'Searching for a Heart.'" Mike held up his hand. "It's not a thing, I just like the tune."

Ernest laughed and Mike half expected him to pull out his notebook and write it down.

"I've always dug 'Werewolves of London,'" Ernest said.

"Then can you tell me what the hell that song is about?"

"No idea."

"You're the worst. Why was I referred to you again?"

"The government likes cheap."

"They didn't pay you to follow me, did they? As you can see, I've already got someone on my tail."

"Are you considering asking her out?"

"I feel if I answer that question, I'm going to get an invoice tomorrow," Mike said.

Mike's hand started shaking. He didn't notice it at first because his mug was empty and he still hadn't eaten anything. He knew he was in real trouble when the tremors reached his elbow. The diner's sweet symphony of assorted languages, whitewashed porcelain plates meeting cheap metal tables, and fry cooks flirting with waitresses coalesced into a high-pitched whine that threatened to lacerate his eardrums. Mike could see Ernest's concerned expression, but he knew if he didn't use whatever motor skills he had left, he wouldn't make it to the bathroom. He sloppily exited the booth, slurred incoherently, and took three long strides past the counter.

Mike lowered his shoulder through the bathroom door, sank to his knees, and lifted the seat without studying its condition. He violently threw up a mix of half-digested coffee and medication. The sight of it made him vomit even more. He emptied himself out, but his body refused to believe it. Dry heave after dry heave forced his head further into the bowl. It felt as if all his ribs were cracking. The ringing in his ears was deafening. He wept as hard as he was throwing up.

Mike's body finally began to accept he had nothing left to give. He swallowed hard, forcing down whatever stomach acid had been on its way up. He flushed the toilet and collapsed.

He felt drunk as if he had spent the morning chasing gin and tonics with rotgut whiskey. He could hear a voice shouting at him. Phil. His brother was trying to open her door. He kept telling Mike to be quiet.

Mike's deployment date was close. Phil had decided his brother needed a sendoff that would require a liver transplant. Mike drank every shot handed to him and smoked a cigar every hour. A cheap champagne fight broke out, which added a layer of suds.

Phil lost his grip on Mike, whose head slammed against the door. He didn't feel anything and tried to drunkenly explain that there was a trick to the lock. He didn't get a chance to try it. She was standing in front of them with a baseball bat in her hands. She thought someone was breaking in. The rest of the men scattered.

Mike fell into her arms and then immediately hit the floor. She didn't have the upper body strength to catch him. She made him crawl to the bathroom, poking him with the end of the bat to keep him moving. Mike managed to slide into the tub before she dumped a gallon of ice water on his head. He lost his breath and started crying. All of his insecurities and fear rushed out.

"Why are you with me?" he asked. "You could be with anyone. Why did you choose me? You can run away after I leave. Don't wait for me. I love you too much to see you waste your time. I don't want to die. I want to stay here with you. Why are you with me?"

"Because I love you," was her answer to most of his questions.

The others she ignored. She was his forever, and he couldn't believe it fully. All her love didn't seem possible.

Didn't she harbor some kind of unrequited love for someone? How could she possibly love him with her whole heart?

He was laid out like a starfish thinking about all this when she returned hours later to dredge him out of his emotional waste.

"Get up," she said. "Get up and I'll figure out a way to make it all go away."

She may have only said it once, but Mike heard it on repeat.

Get up.

Get up.

Get up.

Mike shouldn't have looked at himself in the mirror. His cheeks were hollowed out, and he was the color of a Styrofoam cooler. He didn't have the strength to splash water on his face, so he unlocked the door and rejoined the world.

His breakfast companions hadn't left.

"You want to talk about it?" Ernest asked.

"Not until I'm legally obligated."

"He's fine," he said to Nikki.

Mike didn't want to face her, but he did. The cloth she pressed to his forehead was cold, but her smile was warm.

"Welcome back," she said.

7.

Mike needed shaving cream.

He had been using soap and water for weeks since prematurely trashing his last purchase. His skin was getting raw. He could have asked Phil for some, but it had been awkward since Mike had saved him from flames that hadn't actually existed. The only good thing that came out of the whole scenario was that Phil's wife and son moved back in.

Mike considered banning shaving altogether. Would have been a hell of a lot easier. He looked good with a beard, but she used to hate it. A beard meant she wouldn't kiss him. He couldn't live without her lips until he had to.

Deep fall had set in, so he knew the ducks would be gone. He glanced at the front counter on his way in and was proven correct. He walked down the center aisle, confident he would escape this trip unscathed.

They didn't have his preferred brand. He eyed the cheapest one and noticed soap was on sale.

Do I need soap? he thought. *I'm still showering, right?*

A guy in line started chatting up the women in front of him. Mike's ears homed in and heard him deliver a line that would have made Bill Clinton blush. The woman was visibly offended. Her voice sounded familiar. Sure enough, it was Nikki, who had a young kid with her. She hadn't mentioned him. He could be a nephew. Either way, considering how well their last meeting went, he didn't blame her.

Mike watched the guy back off. She wasn't in any trouble and didn't appear to see him.

Small miracles, he thought. *Now, do I want Alpine Shower or Misty Springtime?*

That's when it jumped him.

Mike started to see numbers form, but they didn't mean anything. They appeared one at a time. Over and over again. The sequence didn't add up. He wasn't looking at a birthday, anniversary, or an online password.

He shut his eyes. He thought he heard shouting but couldn't tell if it was part of the episode or reality. It sounded like an ambush or tactical strike. Each shout he heard sounded like hot metal striking flesh.

"Wake up, soldier," Mike said.

He was in his apartment, which was a mess. The table was set, but dinner was abandoned on the stove. Deep pink lipstick rimmed an empty wine glass. He heard laughter coming from his bedroom. He had a towel wrapped around his waist. He followed the trail of discarded clothing. He pushed the bedroom door open and found her curves ensconced underneath a slim sheet.

"Hey," she said.

"You're not real," Mike said.

"You keep saying that, but I keep showing up."

"I needed to get shaving cream. And now I'm here."

"Take off your clothes and get back in this bed."

"I'm only wearing a towel."

"My lucky morning. Not too many of those left. Get into the bed and bring that with you."

His towel had parted.

"I want us to do it 343 times. You're not going to stop until I tell you to."

"What did she say?" Mike asked out loud.

He was halfway back in reality. He could see her in the bed in the paper supplies aisle. He could reach out and touch her hips next to a 12-pack of toilet paper.

She gestured to him to lie down. She never wanted him to leave the bed. But there were postseason baseball games to watch, a fantasy football team to manage, bank accounts to worry about, affairs to get in order before basic training. All she needed was for him to be next to her and he kept putting it off. He always walked into a comatose lover buried underneath every blanket he had. He'd squeeze her firmly, reclaim a square of the comforter, and fade to sleep adamant that he'd make it all up to her the following night. It never happened. He ran out of tomorrow nights.

"Did I stutter?" she asked. "How are you going to follow orders when you can't hear shit? Or are you embarrassed because I caught you checking out that woman at the diner?"

"I was just being friendly. I'm only human."

"What could she possibly have that I don't?"

She threw the sheet off the bed. Her skin was illuminated like a soft white light bulb. She moved slightly so her ass was in full view, and then lay flat on her back. She fully opened her legs.

"How much wine did you have without me?" she asked. "I said make love to me, silly. Maybe I'll break you, and you won't have to leave."

"The Army would probably draft you instead."

"I'm too much to handle," she said. "Stop wasting time. Let's get to it. I want my 343."

343, Mike thought.

3.

4.

3.

The numbers.

They came one after another again, slowly this time.

3.

4.

3.

343.

His draft number.

The woman ahead of him in line for the movie was reciting a telephone number. His brother's clock had been stopped at 3:43. All those baseball stats at the diner must have included a three, a four, and a three. The soap was three for $4, and the shaving cream was three bucks. His change from his first pharmacy visit was $3.43. It had never been the ducks.

Son of a bitch, Mike thought.

His mind flipped solidly into the present and started working on a new callus for his newly discovered wound.

"He's got a gun!"

The screaming hadn't been an illusion. The customers in the aisles had hit the ground. Those by the registers were catatonic. The guy from before had Nikki's arm in a vise grip. His other hand held a .38 Special snub nose. He had it pointed at the cashier. His speech was slurred, his clothes were dirty, and his hair was unwashed. Mike could see the outlines of the guy's dog tags in the back pocket of his fraying khakis. Maybe Mike knew him over there. The man had come home and lost his way. Or maybe it was the other way around. The danger was real this time.

"Sir, please drop the gun," Mike said.

The man lowered the weapon to his hip and turned his head just enough to survey his new enemy with his peripheral vision. He shoved Nikki away.

Mike felt pretty dumb. He was unarmed and was putting a crowd of people at more risk. He hadn't consciously raised a fist in anger since he arrived back home. The only advantage he had was that this guy still had his back to him.

The guy's elbow flinched and his right foot moved just enough for Mike to figure out he had made up his mind to shoot.

Mike's forearm disrupted his aim but didn't disable his trigger finger. A bullet tore through Mike's right bicep. There was more screaming. Mike ignored the pain and threw his left fist into the guy's face. The robber dropped immediately. The gun discharged again, but the stray bullet only shredded a bag of cheese puffs. Mike picked up the gun and emptied out the rest of the ammo. He walked calmly to the hardware section and grabbed an extension cord. He turned the former soldier over on his stomach and tied his hands. The threat had been neutralized.

"You can call the police now," Mike said to the cashier.

She yelped but picked up the phone. Mike felt hungry and a little lightheaded.

"There's a lot of blood, so she should call the paramedics too," Nikki said.

She was right. His shirtsleeve was bright red.

"Thanks," he said.

Once the paramedics arrived, they stopped the bleeding and bandaged Mike's arm. They told him to stay put until they gave him a final once over after they checked out some of the older customers who were finally calming down. The cheese puffs hadn't made it.

Nikki's kid stared at him, trying to get the courage to ask something.

"Did it hurt?"

Mike shrugged.

"Just bad luck with a bullet," he said.

"Were you a soldier over there?"

Mike nodded.

"Well, thanks for saving my mom," the kid said.

"Sure thing. How old are you?"

"Ten."

"You like school?"

"No."

Mike laughed.

"Just don't join the Army," he said.

The kid made a face that clearly showed his frustration with yet another adult telling him what to do. Mike could see Nikki giving the police officer an earful. She was going to press charges up the ass.

His body started freaking out, starting from the pit of his stomach. He was going to throw up all over this kid. Or throw him through the automatic door.

A worried survey of his immediate surroundings found his draft number missing. The cop's badge number was a mix of fives, sevens, and nines. All the price tags in the area were out of sight. None of the promotional signage featured a three, four, or three. The kid was the only person within a foot of him.

The kid.

Fuck me, he thought. *He's ten. Three plus four plus three.*

Mike flashed back to a peach orchard.

She stood up and proudly showcased a small peach. She held it close to her smile. Norman Rockwell would have had a field day.

The present returned. Mike decided not to wait for the paramedics and resolved that growing a beard was a safer alternative.

The kid stared at him awkwardly again.

"Take it easy," Mike said.

Cherry on Top

"Sir, I'm afraid we can't allow you to check in," the hotel clerk said.

Carl's shoulders sagged.

"Is there something wrong with my reservation?" he asked.

"No, everything is quite in order. However ..."

"What?"

Carl's patience in unearthing Canadians' supposedly famed hospitality was finally spent.

"The card you supplied is short of funds."

Actually, Carl thought, *it has no funds thanks to the outrageous sixty-dollar cab ride from the airport.*

"Who cares?" he asked. "I'm a guest lecturer, a bookish author to boot, not a rock star. There'll be no incidentals, I assure you."

"Company policy, sir. I simply can't allow it."

The man handed Carl back his debit card and then retreated to a back office. It was past midnight, so Carl was alone in the ornate lobby. He shuffled to one of the long plush couches out of view of the main desk. He turned his lone suitcase on its side and unzipped the fraying zipper. Carl rifled through the pile of semi-clean clothes and pulled out the pair of jeans he had worn last night during the worst dinner of his life. The back pocket still held the last cash he had; fifty dollars his ex-girlfriend had gifted him after she informed him their latest dumpster fire of an affair was over.

"Fuck," Carl mumbled.

He wouldn't have felt so low if he hadn't paid for dinner. Or let her stay at the apartment he was about to be evicted from. Or felt tenderness and warmth when she sleepily hugged him in the night. Or cried after she woke, laughing that she had confused him for her boyfriend. Or arrived at the airport early the next morning only to remember he had booked an evening flight. Or navigated back to his apartment by public transit to find her smoking weed with his pantless, hipster roommate.

Carl trudged back over to the reception desk, the cash firmly wadded up in his fist. He chided himself for accepting the speaking engagement invitation from the University of Toronto. Professor William Redmapleleaf—or whatever the fuck his name is, Carl thought—had caught him during a vulnerable moment. His second novel wasn't selling in the States, or anywhere else for that matter, and he vowed to kill himself if good news didn't present itself immediately. His eviction notice arrived soon after he hung up with the good professor, so the universe came pretty close to offing him.

Despite being housed in a beautiful brick building, the hotel's lobby featured an overabundance of ceiling-to-floor mirrors that reflected Carl's swollen middle-aged frame and bubbling foreigner anger. He watched himself take every step, hating his tightening blue jeans and broken black loafers. He couldn't stand his ring of hair, aggressively planning the rest of its hurried retreat, or his battered teeth, yellowed from his mistaken assumption that coffee and cigarettes were keys to recapturing the magic of his writing career. He could only claim pride in his hands, which were veined, tough, masculine. Women remarked on them well after dismissing the rest of what he had to offer, and they did their job admirably whenever one of those ladies lost whatever pride she had clung to before the onslaught of Manhattans or pills. Plus, Carl also could turn a phrase, each word unlocking the desperation women usually kept locked away from men like him.

He stopped in the middle of the lobby to calm himself. However, Carl pictured his promiscuous junkie ex, whose stringy blond hair and heroin track marks were likely occupying his roommate's pullout bed. He never should have let that degenerate into the apartment—*goddamn the man's rent money*, Carl thought, *and all the miserable narcotics I bought with it*. He considered using the money to buy a hot meal—surely it would be his only meal, based on his current financial state—and sleeping on the surprisingly clean streets with the rest of the Canadian bums.

"My name is in the registry," Carl grunted. "That's got to mean something in this Tim Horton's of a country!"

He pressed and held the service button illuminated on the front desk. He hoped it sounded like a New Orleans funeral in the back office. The Molson-swilling, bucktoothed Canuck staggered back out, looking as if Carl had interrupted him from whatever passed for Canadian sitcom hijinks.

"I see you're still here," the man said.

"Considering the University of Toronto paid for a room, I demand to sleep in it!" Carl yelled.

"No need to resort to shouting. You know the policy. I can't help you."

"Do you accept bribes in this part of the world?" Carl asked, throwing his fifty dollars at the man's ill-fitting blazer.

"I'm assuming this is U.S. currency," he said.

The man picked up the wrinkled bill without losing eye contact with Carl. He rubbed it in his hand, grimacing after he discerned his assumption was correct.

"You'll have to exchange this before I can accept it."

"And where the hell am I supposed to do that at this hour?"

"The airport."

"Now listen, I did exchange some money when I got off the plane, but I was robbed by one of your disreputable cabbies. I know he took a longer route here! I'm giving you the last cash to my name, so let me in the goddamn door or I'm going to stage a Twitter revolt against your hotel that will leave the owner's children penniless and destitute."

"I'm sorry, sir, are you imbalanced in some way?"

"I assure you I am quite balanced. To suggest otherwise is unprofessional and rude. I'd like you to please solve my dilemma."

"One moment, please."

Carl maniacally ripped the folded bill from the clerk's hand.

"I'm not letting this out of my possession until we resolve this!" Carl shouted.

The stunned Canadian bowed meekly as he stumbled back to his office. Carl reached over the counter and shoved the man's pen off the desk. He cracked his elbow on the computer screen, which swiveled and pushed a sheaf of papers toward the floor. Carl tried in vain to corral the pile but couldn't stop the sheets from snowflaking their way to the carpeted floor. He surveyed the mess wearily and then tiptoed away.

Carl had the sudden urge to call his ex. She'd undoubtedly be awake. She might answer the phone while some unsuspecting heathen had one of her legs wrapped around her head—as she had done in the past—but she might be willing to wire him some money after faking yet another orgasm. She had vacuumed most of Carl's first advance into her nose, so she rightly owed him. And if not for that, then for the abortion he had recently financed despite not being her sperm donor. Carl's anger burped again, but he swallowed it, remembering that not only was his phone dead, but he had neglected to set up his international calling plan. Much like his checking account and his ex, his phone was a deflated life raft.

And then Carl actually burped. He felt goose bumps as stomach acid washed up against the back of his throat. The dollar tacos he had purchased from a greasy stand under the 30th Avenue subway station in Astoria barked in his colon. He hunched over as stomach pains threatened to pull him to the ground.

No, no, no, no, no, he thought. *Please, not now.*

Carl's bowels hadn't been right since he had developed an on-again, off-again relationship with prescription pills. He'd know in another minute whether he had time to wait for the clerk to decide his fate or if this situation demanded the nearest porcelain depository. Carl slowly stood upright, walked a few steps toward the front desk. He haltingly inhaled. A smirk had barely creased the corner of his lips when he felt his asshole giving way to whatever terror lurked inside his intestinal tract.

Carl clenched heroically just as the man returned to his abandoned post.

"Sir, I think I have a solution," he said, ignoring the clutter at his feet. "We're going to hold that money as collateral. In the morning, please have someone affiliated with the university stop by so that we can run a credit card to ensure we receive payment for any damages. Any resistance to this idea will force us to remove you from the premises. Would this be amenable to you, sir?"

"Yes, yes, fine, I'll sign whatever," Carl said. "Just kindly give me my room key and I won't bother you anymore this evening."

The man scratched out a makeshift contract on a piece of hotel stationery, which Carl signed while jogging in place.

"Are you okay, sir?" The clerk asked.

"I'll suffer no more questions from you," Carl responded. "Key, please."

The man held his hand out and flexed his fingers.

"I'll have that fifty now."

Carl felt a silent fart escape. Defeated, he dropped the limp bill into the clerk's hand. He was rewarded with a silver key attached to a large keychain engraved with the number "575."

"Real keys, huh?"

"Yes sir, it makes our guests feel distinguished," the man said, shuffling his papers back into a uniform stack. "But I don't expect someone like you to appreciate Old World charm."

"One more word from you and I'll ... Jesus Christ!" Carl shouted as his stomach twisted and rumbled. "I'll deal with you in the morning!"

Carl quickly gathered his luggage and sprinted toward the elevators. He paused in front of the lobby's restroom. His germophobic tendencies normally prevented him from using public bathrooms, however, the digested tacos may not be patient enough to ride the elevator five floors. He took a napkin out of his pocket, wrapped it around the door handle, and yanked. The door didn't budge.

"Sorry, the lavatory is only open during daytime hours," the clerk yelled from the front desk.

Carl didn't have time for a response. He continued power walking to the elevators. Instead of a row of closed, aluminum doors, Carl found a group of men surrounded by all manner of equipment and electrical parts standing in front of six open doors.

"I hope you're not on a top floor, man, because these babies are going to be out all night," one of the repairmen said.

"Where are the stairs?" Carl asked, each syllable stoking the brimstone traveling up his throat.

"That way," the guy said, pointing in the opposite direction.

Carl took a moment to let everything settle inside him momentarily and then ran back across the deserted lobby. He barged into the door leading to the stairs and leaped two stairs at a time. He tuckered out as he neared the fourth floor. He felt the flow of shredded meat, cheese, and sour cream slide ever closer to his damp underwear. His luggage slipped from his hand and barreled down the stairs. He slumped up against the wall and whimpered. He stood motionless far longer than the situation warranted. Thoughts of giving up and defecating in the stairwell crept into his fatigued mind.

The moment he summoned the courage to start moving again, the lights went out. Sure that they operated on some kind of motion sensor, Carl weakly waved his arm in the darkness, but he wasn't making enough movement to trigger them. He dropped to his knees—*I can't risk falling in the dark*, Carl thought. *Someone would surely find me soiled and bloody*—and started to crawl up the remaining flight of stairs. His head crashed into the door to salvation and he stood stoically, feeling the running faucet of sweat down his back chill with a vague promise of reaching the summit. The lights snapped back on just as Carl opened the door and stepped into the fifth-floor hallway.

He had to blink away moisture from his eyes when he saw that his room two steps away.

"I'm going to make it!" Carl yelled. "Toronto isn't so bad after all!"

He calmly, confidently strutted the short distance and felt nothing but bliss as the key slid effortlessly into the lock. He smiled, feeling relief swell into his gut. He turned the key in one swift motion.

Crack.

"What the ..." Carl murmured. He looked down as the stubby end of the key dropped out of his fingertips. The business end of the key was still lodged in the lock.

"No!" Carl screamed. "Oh my, I'm going to shit myself. This is it. Well, I tried my best. I suppose, try as one might, one doesn't always make it. Thirty-three years accident-free is a good run. How do I do this? Do I just let go? Maybe my body won't allow it to happen."

He unclenched for a moment, realizing that nothing was going to stop this shit hurricane.

"I'm not ready yet! Just give me a moment to remember this as the last moment before my life officially turned brown. Where will I dispose of this disaster after it happens? How will I call the front desk and explain this? It's all their fault, really. This uptight establishment forced me into this precarious position! This feces is on their hands!"

A door opened across the hall. A short woman in a soft white robe walked out and put her arm on her hip.

"What is the meaning of all this dreadful commotion?" she asked.

Carl didn't hesitate. He pushed her aside and bounded into her hotel room. He raced through the open bathroom door, unlatching his belt at the same time. His pants were barely past his knees as he hovered over the toilet.

Who knows what kind of germs this woman has, Carl thought as he violently emptied himself.

"Excuse me, what the hell do you think you're doing?" the woman asked, holding her nose and closing the bathroom door. "My god, you smell terrible."

"I'm so sorry about this," Carl said. "My key broke off as I was about to enter my room. You saved my life. I owe you!"

"I'm calling the front desk and then the authorities! You can't violate someone's privacy in this manner. I'm going to have to switch rooms, that smell will never go away!"

"I promise to flush multiple times," Carl said while depressing the handle for the first time. "I'm sure the cleaning staff is more efficient than this hotel's reception employees!"

"How much did you have to bribe them to let you in here, you monster?"

My dignity, fifty bucks, ruptured colon, Carl thought.

"I'm a visiting dignitary if you have to know. I'm here promoting my new book. I'm just having an extremely bad day that has improved immensely thanks to this commode."

"Please hurry up. My husband will be returning any moment from a business function and I won't have him thinking I'm having an affair with the likes of you."

A final gurgle exited Carl and he sighed happily.

"That should be the end of it!" he yelled to his new friend.

"I can do without the play-by-play," she said. "What's your name?"

Carl hesitated, unsure if he should reveal his true identity in case the woman changed her mind about calling the police. Then again, she could be a fan, which would go a long way to settling this mess. He told her.

"Not the author by that name?" she asked.

"The same!"

"Well, I was quite disappointed with your second novel. The characters in your first novel were bursting with life, and your dialogue was so tender. Your new one features a bunch of cardboard cutouts humping each other like stray pets."

Carl would have loved to explain the nuances in his recent prose, however, he had discovered a mound of shit that had missed the toilet and splattered on the black-and-white-tiled floor. After her comment, he stopped wiping it up with a thin piece of toilet paper and started cleaning the brown pile with a bra hanging up behind the door.

"All criticism is good criticism!" Carl said, dumping the soiled undergarment in the trash.

"You've been in there long enough," she replied. "I'm calling the front desk."

"Please do," he said, walking out of the bathroom and closing the door behind him. "And could you let them know about my broken key? Tell them I plan on lodging a formal complaint in the morning. Thanks again for your hospitality in my time of need."

Carl could feel his stomach regaining its former, relaxed shape as he went back to the stairwell to retrieve his luggage. It had opened, predictably, and his phone sat shattered on a lower step. Carl left it there and shoved everything else back into the bag. After returning to the now quiet hallway, he sat up against his room's door, feeling the old sweat in his clothes rub against his skin.

He cursed his ex with his last conscious thought before closing his eyes and falling asleep.

The following afternoon, Carl dumped a half-eaten chicken finger into the red basket in front of him. The gray meat crawled out of its beige shell, seemingly hell-bent on drowning itself in the placid pool of ranch dressing. Carl grimaced disgustedly and washed his mouth out with a hearty slug of flat fountain soda.

From his counter stool at the university's student-run diner, he jealously eyed the coiled line at the gourmet taco stand on the opposite side of the student union. A cardboard burrito in a sombrero coldly stared back at him. Carl opted for this dump, which had all the charm and quality food of a Little League complex's snack shack, because Mel's Mexican Cantina forced you to pay the perspiring, out-of-breath whale manning the cash register immediately after the sun-deprived Canadian imp shoved meat, salsa, and cheese into a warm tortilla. The diner's inattentive table service allowed for an inspired dash-and-deal meal scheme.

Carl's plan included running into his waiter hurriedly, clearly distraught by a pressing phone call from the university president. He imagined Canadians were too polite to pursue anyone for reparations, and certainly not a man of his occupational pedigree. Besides, it appeared as though the diner's staff had its hands full with the lower class, homeless vagabonds impersonating intellectual college students. Even if he was caught, Carl couldn't imagine the humiliation being any harsher than the torment he had endured this morning.

Luckily, there had been an early morning conference at the hotel. Carl managed to avoid the front desk and gorge himself on soggy fruit and sour coffee at the free buffet. He had exited a lecture halfway through, more than enough time to justify absconding with a blueberry muffin, and quite literally ran into the university director responsible for his sordid Canadian misadventure. Carl had noisily devoured his baked good while engaging the fellow in an intellectually intense debate about the role of linear time in post-modernist short story writing. He had wiped crumbs from his wrinkled button-down as the director hailed a cab, oblivious to the man's revulsion at Carl's manic state. Finally remembering his bothersome obligation to the hotel, Carl had grabbed the man by the arm, pulled him from the cab, and ushered him to the front desk like a mousing feline proudly displaying her victim.

The corporate drone from the night before wasn't on shift, depriving Carl of the satisfaction of being vouched for by a decent member of Canadian society. He had been replaced by a faux-tanned pixie with neon-whitened teeth and a perfectly tightened blond ponytail.

"May I present to you Professor ...," Carl had said, forgetting the man's name.

"Roy."

"Hello, sir! My last name's Roy!" the woman had exclaimed, proudly tapping on her gold-plated nametag. "Do you know Emile Roy? He's my grandfather and lives outside Ottawa."

"This is very much beside the point," Carl had interjected. "One of your employees rudely prevented me from checking in last night, and I'm here to right his wrong. Professor Roy has generously agreed to swipe his credit card so that I'm not labeled a squatter."

"I most certainly did not agree to any such thing!" Professor Roy had said. "What is the meaning of this?"

"Allow me to explain fully," Carl had said. "I shifted funds to a variety of different accounts before I set off on my trip and brought a card that is temporarily devoid of funds. Hotel management did not allow me to enter my room when I arrived last night after midnight despite the fact the university graciously paid for my lodging."

"That's right, sir!" Hotel Roy had said. "Everything on my screen says there were no issues during your check-in process."

"Excuse me?" Carl had said, finally releasing his grip on Professor Roy's arm. The man took the opportunity to walk briskly back to the taxi stand.

"Yes, sir. There isn't a note on your reservation or anything."

"What about the money I put up as collateral?"

"Money?"

"I gave the man at the desk last night fifty U.S. dollars so that I could settle into the guest room that is rightfully mine. If there is no note, where is my cash?"

"Let me check with my manager."

"I swear to god, miss, if you go into that back office and come out without my money, I'm liable to call the authorities."

"I'll get to the bottom of this!" Hotel Roy had said, bounding away unperturbed by Carl's warning.

She had found his cash, but there wasn't a note that confirmed it belonged to him. She couldn't release it until she spoke to the night manager, who wouldn't be on duty until later in the afternoon. Carl had shaken his head dejectedly and asked for directions to campus.

Carl still felt the ache in his feet from the five-mile walk. He obviously didn't have money to take a cab and had blown his chance to share one with the director who had knowingly abandoned him. He had arrived at his ill-attended reading with a much larger hole in his shoe and a sweat-soaked shirt. He didn't recite his prose so much as shout at the few semi-interested souls leaning back in their plastic folding chairs. Probably obligated to be there by some prick of an English teacher who assigns his own trashy textbooks, Carl thought and is obviously so jealous of my success, he only required his failing students to attend.

It didn't matter now. He finished the last meal, the last one he'd eat for some time in any country and walked away without bothering to fake an act of rebellion.

"Hey!" a voice boomed.

Carl froze.

"You're that writer campus is buzzing about, right?"

"You must have the wrong person," Carl said, turning his head over his shoulder just far enough to see a white hulk perched precariously on the narrow counter stool next to his abandoned one. "Only a handful of students showed up to my lecture."

"Dude, teenagers don't show up to crap they actually like in the middle of the day. You got to go prime time."

"Well ..."

"Oh shit, man, you were about to blow this place, weren't you?" the large man said, wiping his overgrown paws on a small, shredded napkin. "Shit, sorry, I just couldn't resist saying hello to another artist."

"It's quite all right," Carl said, nervously easing himself back into his seat. "I didn't mean to snap. I haven't had a pleasant trip. Obviously. I wasn't headed anywhere. Just stretching my legs. I'm Carl."

"Bleached Molasses."

"Did I not just finish telling you that I'm out of sorts? Don't add to it by making up a silly name to pester me further!"

The hulk's laugh bellowed, turning more than a few heads.

"You need to lighten up. It's not the world's fault your second novel sucked. Yeah, I read it. Charles, your characters weren't just awful people, they were awfully written. I didn't give two shits about them. And if you don't have a plot, and that turd didn't have a plot to piss on, at least give me some meaty people to chew on while I'm gutting through it. See, rapping is different."

"You're a rapper! What do you know about art and literature? And I said my name is Carl!"

"Carl. Well, I knew it started with C. I just met you. You're a grown man, don't be so fussy about people getting your name right. Rapping is art like anything else—as close to a fusion of literature and music as there is."

"And people know who you are, Mr. Bleached Asshole?"

"Ha!" the rapper said. "See, there you go. Yeah, man, me and my boys were at the Blue Jays game last night and we were mobbed the whole time. Helps that the team sucks moose balls, but still, we'll take it."

"Seriously?"

"Hell no, but you believed me, right? No one knows me this far south. I'm from way up north."

"There's more north above here?"

"First time to Canada?"

"As an adult, yes."

"I'll go easy then. Yeah, there's more north. More wildlife than people, but Canada isn't just the cities closest to your country. I'm trying to branch out and become a Canadian Eminem. I was raised right—my parents loved me, those fuckers—so I've had to nuke my adulthood so I could write about hard times, you know."

"How does one go about doing that?"

"Not by hanging around clean-cut literature types, I can tell you that, pal. Listen, can you like my Facebook page? I'm trying to build up my social media cred."

"I'm afraid I'm not on social media."

"Seriously?"

Carl didn't have much use for the Internet. Why would he willingly log on and be faced with all of the emails from his agent pleading for pages Carl didn't have? Ignoring phone calls and voicemails was so much easier and more refined. Not to mention, the last time Carl had Googled something—his ex's name—he unearthed a website featuring his former lover nakedly writhing on a large Hispanic man's face. The pills he took to get over that little discovery knocked him out for two days.

"No wonder your crap doesn't sell, man, you've got to get on that," the rapper said. "Don't move. I dropped something."

"What?"

Carl felt a pile of powder land on his knee. The rapper glanced around and then bent over, quickly sniffing it up.

"How dare you!" Carl silently yelled. "Did you just do a line of cocaine off my leg?"

"Yeah, lot easier doing a bump like that rather than sneaking it in the bathroom. These Canadian college kids are monsters. They'd break the door down, steal my stash, knife me, and do lines off my corpse. Fucking animals."

"Does the cold weather zap all your brains or something? What kind of behavior is this?"

"Shit, you're right, where are my manners," the rapper said. "You want some?"

Carl thought for a moment. He hadn't done coke in some time. Pills, sure, plenty of pills. He pictured his trampy ex sucking on the crack pipe she loved more than him, devouring the smoke while happily ignoring his needs.

"That's very generous of you," he said. "Maybe just one."

The rapper slapped him on the back and dumped a thin line of powder on his own thigh. Carl made a show of dropping the remnants of a chicken finger on the floor beneath them.

"Bro, pick that up, you slob," the rapper said, winking.

Carl bent over as Bleached Mayonnaise—*I'm certainly under no obligation to remember his name accurately*, Carl thought—put his beefy arm on Carl's shoulder to block him from view. The cocaine felt like napalm ripping apart a jungle up his nose. Carl raised his snout just above the rapper's leg and smiled contently.

"Heh, look at those two fags," someone snickered behind them.

From his current position just above his new drug buddy's crotch, Carl watched the rapper's eyes narrow.

"You fucking kids!" the rapper yelled, shoving Carl out of the way and off his stool. Carl smacked his head on the linoleum, causing a dull bell to chime next to the synthetic techno hell in his brain. The rapper grabbed the teenager's popped collar and brought him closer.

"I rap about this shit. It's called intolerance. You heard of that in your bullshit classes? Jesus, we got plenty of gays in Canada. We're supposed to be nice, dammit."

"I'm from Kansas," the student whimpered, frightened by the blood starting to trickle out of the rapper's nose.

"You don't see me walking around making jokes about you fucking cattle, do you? People are fucking people, man. Leave them alone. Get out of my sight, sheep fucker."

A crowd had gathered by the time Carl wobbled to his feet. He witnessed a thick, neckless man parting the onlookers, his fist raised. Carl's warning shout came out as a lazy whisper. The man cold-cocked the rapper, who lost his grip on the ignorant student. Blood and remnant coke dust gushed down the rapper's face as he collapsed. A group of amped up bullies started kicking and punching the downed hulk who had been so giving of his drugs.

"Ahhhhhh!" Carl yelled, his arms outstretched, his fists balled tightly.

He jumped on the back of the lout closest to him and started scratching out his eyes with his ragged, dirty fingernails. The wriggling human beneath him unleashed a high-pitched whine and tried to shake Carl off him. To his credit, Carl wrapped his thin arms around the boy's neck and squeezed with all the cocaine-infused strength he could muster. The chokehold did its job admirably, buckling the man's knees. He lost consciousness and fell backward. Carl, too proud of his achievement to realize what was happening, once again cracked his head on the floor.

This time, his lights went out.

"What say you buy me a drink?" the woman sitting next to him at the airport bar asked.

Carl had a bag of ice cubes pressed up against his swollen right eye. His new rapper friend had graciously helped him back to the hotel, slapping concert flyers into the hands of everyone standing in the lobby. Carl refused Molasses's offer to pay for his cab to the airport, unwilling to fall into debt to leave the country and be forced to communicate with that barbarian in the future. He simply thanked his coke-addled protector, rescued his money from the new meathead at the front desk, and fled the premises.

He had walked forty-five minutes through Chinatown to get to the subway station he had located on Google Maps. The subway led him to a bus, which took him the rest of the way to the airport. The maneuver had only cost him three dollars, enabling him to justify buying a drink at one of the airport's bars. He had begged the bartender for a bag of ice once his eye started throbbing again.

"This is the last of my money," Carl told her, shooting down all the bourbon he could afford. It barely wet the inside of his mouth.

"Seriously?"

"Yeah."

"But you're so good looking."

Carl stared down the petite black woman, whose misshapen breasts looked as if they were boarding an earlier flight, sitting next to him. He had barely slept the last two days, his razor hadn't made it across the border, and remnant cocaine dust dotted his faded black trousers.

"I'm an author. Not the best-selling kind."

"That's a shame because you've got some nice lookin' hands."

"Excuse me, miss, are you imbalanced in some way?"

"Where the hell did you learn how to talk to women?"

"Same place I learned to make money, I guess."

"What's the story?"

"I'm not in the mood to tell it."

"Weren't kidding about the crappy writer bit, were you? You're in some kind of mood because your uptuck just turned into a steel teepee."

Embarrassed, Carl discreetly adjusted himself. He watched the woman slowly slurp her gin and tonic out of a thin red straw. He wanted to tell her the alcohol did more to arouse him than she ever would.

"Spill it," she said. "And maybe you'll get to see my tits."

Jesus, Carl thought, *anything but that.*

"I have thirty-some dollars left," he said instead. "It'll work out to just enough to pay for my cab ride back to the apartment that's mine for another twelve hours and for subway fare to get to Grand Central."

"What then?"

"Then I sleep there until I'm dead or, more likely, my agent hunts me down for the pages I owe him. My phone broke, so he'll have to be crafty. Maybe he'll spot me enough money for a dive hotel in Queens if he ever finds me."

"Fucking grim."

"Life of an artist."

"Pft, more like a degenerate."

"Fine line."

The airport's public address system boomed. Flights delayed, weather inclement. Carl eyed his empty glass glumly and considered walking home from LaGuardia so he could order another.

"You seem like a real prick, but I'll make you a deal," she said imploring him to fill in the blank.

"Carl."

"Carl. I'm Cherry."

"No shit."

"Make fun of my name and I'll start screaming *racist*."

"God, what's the deal?"

"If you let me rant about my fuck-stick of a husband, I'll buy you two more rounds. No use being trapped *and* sober."

"I don't have to talk?"

"I'd prefer if you didn't."

Carl scratched the inside of his thigh. The bottom row of cheap Canadian whiskey called to him. The row above, which housed the American-as-missile-defense-and-Walmart-$5-DVDs Kentucky bourbon, bellowed.

"Cherry, that would be just fine."

Black Coffee

I remember darkness.

Never total. Never complete. Just enough to provide nightmares. Or allow your cousin to sleep until noon.

I was, and remain, an early riser. There's nothing I loved more than sleeping over my aunt and uncle's house, but, come on, a guy could go hungry waiting for his teenage cousin to snap out of her heavy slumber. (Of course, I'm failing to acknowledge that I talked her ear off until well into the early morning hours.)

While my eyes opened the moment white-hot sunlight forced itself through the thin blinds, I couldn't just leap out of my sleeping bag and rush out into the wide-awake-for-hours world. Leave the room too early and you'd be forced (yes, in my young mind, I was painfully *forced*) to brush your teeth and be presentable enough to go to church with your aunt and uncle. It's much easier to feign sleep rather than faith.

The church wasn't the same one that my parents sporadically attended, so not only was I bored out of my mind hearing about how Jesus saved the world (not quick enough to prevent himself from being hammered into a board by the Romans), but they didn't follow the same routine! I could never tell if the mass was almost done or not, or if I could sneak out an action figure or two without anyone thinking I was asking for immediate damnation. One time, the priest encouraged all the kids to attend a Sunday school session held during mass. My aunt looked at me and I hope my expression conveyed that if I had to endure the teachings of the Catholic Church, there was no way in hell ... er ... God's infinite eternity that I was going to fake-make new friends at the same time. I'm a good soldier, but there's a limit and that was it. She patted me on the shoulder and said an extra Hail Mary for my introvert soul (I'm assuming).

To avoid all of this, I did what any other heathen pre-teen might do in that situation: I reached for the nearest V.C. Andrews novel on my cousin's floor. (I would have also settled for *The Baby-Sitters Club*, Danielle Steel, or *Goosebumps*. I didn't discriminate.) Just by feeling the raised text on the cover, I could tell the book I found was one of Ms. Andrews' tawdry, incestuous tales. Score!

Alas, I had already read *Flowers in the Attic* cover-to-cover (a fairly traumatic experience for some readers, never mind one who hadn't taken a sex ed class, but I barely flinched at an imprisoned, emaciated brother and sister going at it in a dusty attic). I know I had brought a few Boxcar Children books with me, but those were sitting on the coffee table in the living room—way too early to risk it, church was still a real possibility.

I watched my cousin's New Kids on the Block alarm clock mark the time. It seemed as bored and restless as I was. My cousin and younger brother remained motionless under a pile of homemade blankets we'd stitched together years ago. They were supposed to make you dream about your favorite crush (Punky Brewster) when combined with my cousin's quartz crystal and moody incantations.

I heard a screen door squeal and then slam. My heart pounded but I remained motionless. Many Sunday mornings were ruined by jumping the gun and running headlong into a car still idling in the garage. One had to hear the vehicle scrape the edge of the steep driveway, the gears of the garage door quiet after screeching across the neighborhood and wait five whole minutes before even thinking about making a move. I watched the clock's cartoon-like numbers inch closer to the approved time, unzipping my sleeping bag to prepare for a quick exit.

Finally! Freedom!

I made for the kitchen.

The gray stone floor iced my feet. I tiptoed to the counter, unsure if my aunt had gone to the bakery earlier that morning.

No luck.

I didn't get too down because I knew a glazed donut bounty was sure to arrive once my aunt was done praying for more religious nephews.

The coffeemaker mumbled a few final drops into the nearly empty pot. There was a dark liquid trail leading to a slick stain left behind by a to-go mug. My stomach rumbled as I breathed in the charred smell of spent coffee beans. Coffee was alien to me then, not yet a faithful and nervous companion. I settled for orange juice in a clear plastic cup that had likely been given out as part of a giveaway at a fast-food restaurant or gas station.

One could argue I knew this house better than my own. My cousin was our one and only babysitter every weeknight and during the summer (up to the point where I could take care of myself and my younger brother, surprising as that may be to some). This one-story ranch house just ten minutes away from my parents' split-level had seen more than its fair share of memorable moments. I wrote my first letter on a typewriter set up on the kitchen table I was currently parked at (and had that letter rudely shared across the neighborhood thanks to my cousin); I cried in nearly every forgotten corner of the backyard; I narrowly escaped all of the monsters, murderers, and Darth

Vaders hiding in the basement whenever my aunt asked me to get her a bottle of soda from the extra refrigerator.

I pawed through the open puzzle box to see if I could flush out any of the remaining edge pieces my aunt was hunting for. She always picked the most insanely difficult puzzles—ones that featured similar pastel skies or black-green seascapes and not much else. I sifted through a few hundred pieces as I finished my juice but came up empty. I knew she'd have the whole thing done by the next sleepover. She'd show it off to us, let us break it apart, dump it into the box, and store it in the basement with all the other covered bridges, cow pastures, and descending aircraft. We would help her open the new one but didn't have the attention span to stick around much longer than that. Let's be serious; there were Commodore 64 video games to be played.

I found myself hovering near my grandmother's chair. I should mention here that she wasn't really my grandmother. I also wasn't technically related to anyone in this house by blood (except for my comatose younger brother). Let's just say a lot of death, sadness, forgiveness, and love and other drugs had to break right to congeal our familial bonds. My older brother (whose late mother was my aunt's sister) did all the heavy lifting, briefly shunning one of his elders when they questioned my brotherly legitimacy. A scowling boy standing in the rain just outside my aunt and uncle's property line was all it took for them to say, "Fine, I guess we'll love him too." My aunt gives me the credit for bringing the families together, which, I admit, tickles me because it drives my typically stoic older brother crazy. But he's the glue, now and forever and ever.

The folding tray table next to the chair still houses the candy dish my grandmother used to fill up with M&Ms every morning. I grew up in an era that didn't feature all the cool colors you can find now. (Blue? I mean, what is it with this nonsense?) We had colors, sure, but they were severely outnumbered by the dark brown and tan varieties. Those would always get eaten last, so the dish ended up looking like an unappetizing mass of beige chocolate discs. We'd get desperate though, breaking our "only eat the fun colors" rule. Anyway, the dish was as empty now as the chair. My grandmother's death was the first I truly remembered and understood. I had been too scared to say goodbye to her body. I was scared of everything then. I hope she didn't take offense.

A deep cough and a screen door latch being pulled led me back into the kitchen. I smiled as my aunt walked in carrying a large white box tied up with a thin white string.

"Glazed and crullers," she said, dropping the box on her puzzle. "You the only one up?"

I nodded. I was debating between the two sugary options too intently to respond with words.

"Gonna make more coffee and have a ... break on the porch," she said. "Want to wait for me?"

She could have said cigarette break. It's not like I wasn't going to watch her smoke half a pack while I inhaled a week's worth of sugar next to her.

"Sure," I said.

I watched as she set her glasses back down on her thick hardcover (likely Tom Clancy but could have easily been John Jakes or any number of longwinded fiction writers). The fact that she dressed more casually on the weekends always threw me off. She was a manager at the phone company and came home most nights in shoulder-padded blazers and razor-creased slacks. She was still smartly dressed, mind you, couldn't have the Lord thinking she was a scrub, but she wore her weekend outfits with less misogyny and corporate responsibility bearing down on her.

The coffeemaker did its job, spitting out another four cups. My aunt refilled her mug and motioned toward the front porch.

"Fred!" she yelled.

The *female* mutt poked her head above the arm of the couch she was tucked underneath. (I hadn't realized I had company earlier, probably because I didn't have food to share.) Fred unraveled herself from the tight ball she had worked herself into and stretched. Her tail wagged as my aunt put on the leash she'd wear briefly before being chained to the porch railing. The three of us headed outside with nicotine, caffeine, dog treats, and donuts.

It wasn't a big porch. Just a pile of poured concrete attached to the house that was large enough to have a short wooden bench bolted into it. It served as the perfect perch to watch thunderstorms, shout to the across-the-street neighbors, or argue about whether "Family Matters" or "The Fresh Prince of Bel-Air" was the better show. I plopped down on the front step, my back against the house. My aunt settled in close to the standing ashtray next to the right side of the bench.

"How's school?" my aunt asked, carefully slurping the hot black coffee while ashing her first cigarette at the same time.

I shrugged. (What a little dick. I *loved* school. I could have said anything.)

"Just like your brothers," she sighed.

That much was true.

"Still want to live in New York City when you grow up?" she asked.

"Yep."

"I don't see why. So busy, so dirty. It smells there, you know. And your uncle's brother was propositioned by a hooker. In the Bronx. With his wife right next to him! That was enough for me."

I didn't know what hookers were. Although, maybe I did. Could have been one or two in a V.C. Andrews novel.

"Writers live in New York," I said, a half-eaten glazed donut hanging out of my mouth.

"Oh boy," she said. "You don't want to make money."

I didn't know anything about rent or bills. Or groceries. I wouldn't for a long time.

"What are the odds your younger brother becomes a priest?" she asked. "Be nice to have a priest in the family."

Surely, that was the nicotine talking.

"Don't bet on it," I said, repeating something I heard on television once.

I'm sure I was inhaling a year's worth of secondhand smoke every hour I spent out there, just sitting in silence and watching the neighborhood shake off any Sunday doldrums. Every time she nodded her head toward that side door, I'd follow, Surgeon General's warning be damned. I spent a lot of years and traveled a lot of miles getting back to that front porch.

Which brings us to a U-Haul truck on I-95 North.

"Did you ever think you'd be driving out of New York City with all your crap in a truck and me in the front seat?" my girlfriend asked.

I set my coffee back into the cup holder, watching it slosh over the sides and further stain the cracked gray plastic dashboard.

"Not the way I wrote it up in my head," I said. "But certainly not the worst scenario in the world."

When you spend enough time trying to convince yourself that the wrong people are the right lovers, you grab onto the one you know in your bones you want to make obscenely happy for the rest of your life. Even if they ask you to pack up your life and move to the city where the Red Sox play.

I was done with New York anyway. Or, more accurately, the city was done with me. I had been laid off from the only job I'd ever known and could no longer afford the cramped room in a rats-nest apartment in the bowels of Astoria. Hitting the reset button, even if it meant relocating to northern environs, with the smartest, most beautiful woman I know wasn't the worst idea I've ever had.

"What's up on Twitter?" I asked.

"No news."

"No news? At all? Anywhere?"

"Sorry, I'm sleepy."

"Want to drive?"

"You really want me driving this big truck?"

"Sure, why not."

"I haven't driven in ... I don't know how long. But it's been a while."

"Probably been just as long for me. And I'm under-caffeinated. Speaking of."

I brought the blue, Greek coffee cup to my lips just as we ran over a pothole. Hot brown liquid soaked through my clothes, causing me to utter every curse word public education had taught me.

"How'd that feel?" she asked as I struggled to signal and merge toward the upcoming exit.

I chose to ignore that. More traffic was ahead and I needed a navigator who was actually speaking to me.

The rest of the ride was uneventful if a bit damp. I unloaded everything I owned in the world (which took up less than half the truck), watched my girlfriend drive off an hour later with her mother, headed to my future adopted home, had an ugly cry in the backyard swinging a baseball bat, and fell asleep with three fans pointed at me trying to keep the midsummer heat outside where it belonged.

I woke early. Stupid early. "You're up so early on a Sunday morning at your aunt's house that you're guaranteed a trip to church" early. Of course, thinking about her sparked an idea. I knew she'd be sitting in front of a coffee and paperback right now, same as always.

You want to grab breakfast? I texted.

Three bubbles popped up before I was even done typing.

You pick the place, she replied. *I'm buying. Don't argue.*

I texted her a local favorite that I hoped still existed. I pulled a random assortment of clothes out of my duffel bag, not yet unpacked from yesterday's move. The Neil Young concert T-shirt (ratty as it was) and the pair of cargo shorts I found weren't the same color, which is all I could really ask for.

Hey, you need a ride? My aunt texted me as I headed into the shower.

Ah yes, I hadn't thought about no longer living in a pedestrian nirvana. I couldn't hop on the 6, N, or F trains anymore. Considering both my parents were at work, I was stranded in the burbs.

Sure!

Breakfast and transportation. You're spoiled here already! See you in ten.

She had thinned out, all of the surgeries and other medical shenanigans taking their toll, and her face had a few more creases than the last time I saw her. But she still had that Irish-Catholic fire behind her eyes, that impish laugh employed expertly to make sure you knew there were no hard feelings that she was right and you weren't.

"How are you feeling?" I asked.

"Fine," she said.

"Fine fine or 'I'm full of it' fine?"

"Don't be like my kids," she said, pointing a finger at me. "I'm alive, right?"

"Seems that way."

"I can't eat like I used to, but no one my age does," she said. "Nothing wrong with my ability to drink coffee, so that's good enough. That work for you?"

"You're paying this round, so I surrender."

"This round, huh?"

"Thinking we could make this a regular thing."

"Just us?"

"Well, we could be nice every now and again and invite my father. He looked a little bummed when I told him where I was going. He has Wednesdays off, so maybe we switch up the schedule."

"Can you believe how much I love that guy after he used to call me a jerk-off in high school?"

"My father?"

"Yeah, your father, the saint," she said. "Then he marries my sister. The nerve. Best thing he's ever done is have you boys."

She laughed as she said this. Her love for my father was indestructible. She's right though, having us probably helped.

The salt-and-pepper-haired waitress, who would become an essential part of our breakfast troupe, walked over in military precision, poured out coffees, and started marching back to behind the counter.

"Oh!" she said, turning around. "You two need cream or sugar?"

"Nope, just black. Him too," my aunt said.

"Great, you two holler whenever you're ready," the waitress said.

She had a heavy French accent. We were going to get along just fine.

"Holler!" my aunt yelled, laughing.

"I should have figured! Be back in a jiff. Don't starve in the meantime," the waitress yelled back.

"I like her already," I said.

"She's bringing you coffee and food, of course you do."

"Fair point."

"So. Your *friend* in the White House ain't gonna win it for your *girl*," she said far sooner than I anticipated.

I wasn't going to be sucked into this.

"Well, your *orange pal* is going to be too busy harassing women, shredding civil liberties, and tweeting profanities to get around to all the evil things he's promising if we're dumb enough to elect him," I said.

(Fine, I'm weak. But she started it!)

The political banter didn't last long. We both chuckled at one point, and she lovingly slapped my cheek. That's how we do it (except at Thanksgiving when she's outnumbered—it's not pretty).

"What can I get you two?" the waitress asked.

I'm going to just call her Eva since my memory is too faulty to remember what it actually is/was. That'll make things easier.

"This is my nephew," my aunt said. "He's home from school. New Yorker. He's French too, you know."

"Ah, un autre Français, comment apprécie-tu d'être rentré de l'école?"

A couple of things. I graduated seven years before this conversation. Also, I don't remember even *un peu* from four years of high school French.

"Are you hiring?" I asked.

"He's funny, this one," Eva said. "And no."

"In that case, I'll take a ham and cheese omelet and wheat toast."

"Home fries?"

"Would I be a Frenchman without them?"

"Oui, but not much of one."

"No peppers and onions though. I'll be pushing it enough already after another cup of coffee."

"What can I get for you, darling?"

"Breakfast wrap. I know I won't eat it all, but it's damn good."

"Coming right up. Enjoy that coffee."

I gave her a thumbs up while taking a healthy swig of it. She walked away laughing after slapping me on the shoulder.

"Reading anything good?" my aunt asked.

She skeptically endured all of the nonfiction titles I threw her way, and then she recommended all manner of mysteries and thrillers. She humored me by buying a Richard Russo novel on her Kindle. (She said later that she'd never read anything like that ever again. "It's well written, but I've got my own problems to suffer through, you know? I don't need to read about somebody else's." Well.)

Our food arrived just as I started shaking from the caffeine I'd just ingested on an empty stomach. We fell silent for a bit, in large part because I was shoveling food in an attempt to prevent the coffee from shredding my system.

"Got a plan?" she asked, picking at her meal.

"The beginnings of one. Applied to a few jobs here and in Boston. No replies so far. You hiring?"

"You going to read fiction out loud to me during chemo?" she asked.

"Depends on the pay."

"I have to *pay you*? I helped raise you. You owe *me*, buddy."

"This job interview is not going well. I'll take myself out of the running."

"When you getting married?"

"We've reached the lightning round."

"I'm a sick woman, can you do it soon, please?"

"First of all, that's an admission of how you're feeling, and, second, that's definitely part of the plan."

"She's going to make a beautiful bride. Her family like you?"

"If not, they do an excellent job pretending. Especially considering she's bringing me to their doorstep like a cat with a dead mouse."

"I'm going to wrap this up and have the rest for lunch, and probably dinner," she said, finally putting her fork down. She hadn't eaten much. "That's what happens when you get old. Don't get old."

"I'll see what I can do."

"It's so great that you're home. We all missed you," she said. "Shame none of you turned out to be priests though."

"Got one principal out of the deal. That's close, right."

"He ain't giving us absolution! Detention maybe."

Who can argue with that?

This ended up being our routine every Wednesday for the four months I lived at home. We never talked about the things that were truly hurting us (chemo and doctors for her, unemployment and long-distance love for me). For an hour or so every week, coffee and conversation provided the tonic we needed to survive. We'd change restaurants occasionally and ended up inviting my father and uncle more times than we anticipated. At the tail end of summer, I finally landed a permanent position in Boston. We sat in *our* booth (creatures of habit, my family) and avoided the fact that this was our final breakfast together for a while.

"Let me ask you something," she said.

"Shoot."

"Tom Clancy is dead, right?"

"Yes. Ludlum too. James Patterson might as well be."

"But they still publish books with their names on it."

"Yeah."

"And someone else writes them."

"That's right."

"Well, the authors that do, they gotta be pissed, right? They don't get their own recognition. They're doing all the work! I'd be so mad. They deserve better!"

I laughed, nearly spilling my coffee all over myself (a constant theme in my life if you hadn't noticed).

"Those authors are doing just fine," I said. "They get paid *very* well to write those. A lot of them grew up reading those guys. They'd probably do it for free. Actually, that's probably not true, but it's still an honor to have your name alongside someone like Clancy. Trust me, they aren't bummed about the paycheck."

"Still," my aunt said. "It's BS. All that hard work. You'd never sign up for something like that."

"I could not say yes fast enough. I'd dedicate the first book to you, just to make you upset."

"Well, if you're going to do that, I want it for a book you write, not some zombie Clive Cussler piece of you know what."

"Deal."

"Hey, I know you've got packing to do since you're abandoning us again, but you want to swing by the house? We can have another pot of coffee and I have a stack of old books to give you."

"Considering you're my ride, I can't refuse."

"Good. Think your older brother is visiting today too. Be good to have reinforcements for that crew. We'll wait for them on the front porch."

"You don't still smoke do you?"

She pointed a finger.

"Right, don't be like my cousins, I got it," I said. "But ..."

"Quit a long time ago and look what happened," she said, laughing. "I'm the poster child for healthy living. Let's roll."

I ended up in my usual spot—ass on the top step, head up against the house's white siding—with a pile of beat-up paperbacks that I'm sure included siblings humping.

A few heavy sighs replaced her drags off a cigarette.

"What can you do," she muttered, clearing her throat completely. Louder, she asked, "So am I in your novel?"

"Well, no," I said.

"Pft," she said. "I've been insulted by better people."

As if knowing I needed rescuing, a four-year-old with a blonde ponytail and the grace of a bowling bowl barreled into me.

"Uncle, uncle," she said, her breath coming out in excited gasps. "Boy, do I need to tell you this story."

Her eyes and hands did most of the talking. Out of the corner of my eye, I saw my older brother coming up the front walk with the rest of his brood.

"It's his story to tell," I whispered to my aunt. "Although, keep your eyes on this one."

My niece sensed I wasn't paying attention and put her hands on her hips. She slapped her hands on my cheeks and forced my face to make sure my eyes were looking at her and only her. She then began the story all over again.

My aunt was leaning up against the porch's black metal railing at this point. Her smile was wider than I had seen it in quite some time. My older brother was the real star of this family, even more so with his trio of "I'm smarter than you are and I know it" kids.

Her stance brought back a memory I had forgotten.

My brothers and I all got the chicken pox at the same time. For whatever reason, my aunt had taken us all in and quarantined us in my cousin's room. I remember watching "The Karate Kid" trilogy while trying not to think about the violent itch lurking underneath my Superman pajamas.

My aunt came to check on us frequently since the room was conveniently located next to the front door and her next cigarette break. She'd lean on the doorframe, smacking a pack of Merits against her wrist. She'd pretend to watch Daniel-san crane-kick his way to victory, but I knew her eyes were worrying over the three pockmarked lumps shivering under a motley assortment of blankets. She'd close the door after a while, her fix momentarily winning out over her concern.

I remember darkness.

And pushing against the vinyl roll-up blinds, an orange reminder of what we were missing, the light.

Unkind Bud

The prostitute ended the torturous screwing by slamming Mel's head up against the headboard. His eyes dimmed, but he remained conscious enough to watch the woman, who resembled a freshly unearthed turnip, dismount. She strode to the door wearing only a turtleneck, unashamed of her garbage pail physique. Mel ground his teeth and reached over to the half-spent joint smoldering in the ashtray on the nightstand. He let the ash from the end of the stick fall on the rough, polyester sheets. He had successfully ripped off a hulking suburban mansion left unoccupied by a pair of adulterous bankers early in the evening, and he was fully enjoying his low-class rewards.

Mel had been watching their misdeeds for weeks while traveling around town in a rusted pickup truck, doing odd jobs for bored housewives who needed a few bolts tightened. His marks had gone on vacation, leaving their house in the care of an elderly neighbor, allowing Mel inside after he convinced her the couple had asked for him to repair a few fixtures while they were away. She had made Mel tea while he cracked into a second-floor safe stuffed with cash and jewelry.

He had landed in a bar on the corner of a cobblestone street, staring at his reflection in a hooker's necklace. Her red lipstick distracted him from thinking too hard about the television news report detailing a nearby robbery. He had sniffed his lone finger of bourbon, coughed hard, swallowed the contents of the heavy glass, and felt his ulcer burn. The prostitute had started small talking him, probing to the big ask. It had been a long time since a woman had touched him. There were plenty of men in prison who tried to convince you they looked and felt like women, but their hands, callused and rough, always betrayed them. She had touched his head and immediately pulled her hand away. Mel always wore a buzz cut, trimmed sharp and vicious. The nuns had referenced it, along with his dark eyes and clothes, when fretting over his "black soul." His mother cleaned the rectory, so the family got free room and board right up to the point Mel landed in jail for stealing a holiday collection box and hotwiring the pastor's station wagon. The nuns went from praying for his soul to dismissing it as a lost cause. His mother started eating and never stopped until her heart exploded.

"What, your prick made of wet concrete?" the woman had asked, outstretching her hand as if it were holding a cigarette holder.

"Huh?"

"Jaysis, you're fecking brain dead."

She had rubbed herself hard against Mel's groin long enough to finally get a reaction. He hadn't lasted long, which prompted the hooker to try to violently crack his skull open.

He dozed off. The ringing in his ears intensified as he felt hot ash up against his lips. He tossed the joint on the floor instinctively.

"Gonna fahking light the whore's house on fire, yah ass," Mel said out loud.

He rolled off the bed and stamped out the smoking pile of weed and paper. He held his foot up, massaging away sharp heat and black smudges.

The apartment on the outskirts of the suburbs quieted. Mel thought the woman had gone to the bathroom, but maybe she had left her own place. More likely, she was sitting on her overstuffed couch with her paw in a bag of junk food. He pulled his jeans on and felt for the tight wad of bills in his front pocket. He yanked a twenty out and anchored it under the ashtray. He was overpaying.

Mel retrieved his black T-shirt from a nearby chair and fought himself into it. The weed was taking effect. He giggled, his crime seeming absurd, from a different life. His exit strategy included a quick piss and terse goodbye.

Sure enough, he walked into a dark hallway illuminated only by the flickering television in the living room. Mel skulked into the bathroom, desperate to avoid a conversation until he had his hand on the front doorknob. He tugged at the lightbulb's pull chain.

Mel blinked, stunned.

The walls were washed in blood. It dripped from the shower curtain and puddled on the torn bathmat. His bare feet slipped on a spongy material he could only assume was brain matter. He dropped to a knee, feeling red ooze seep through his dark jeans. He vomited on the closed, bloody toilet seat, adding to the stench that bullied its way into his nostrils and down his throat. He spat, collected himself, and stumbled to the sink.

The water had been left on, a small, steady stream pushing past the pool of blood in the basin. Shaking, Mel turned the faucet on full blast and watched the plasma flake off the white porcelain in chunks. He forced his hand under the water and looked up at the bulb that discharged light through splotches of pink fluid. His hand reached out courageously and wiped away a mass of hair and blood stuck to the bathroom mirror.

"No," Mel said, seeing his reflection.

He wore a black ski mask. His left hand held a knife. He eyed a pale foot sticking out from underneath the shower curtain.

"Don't be fahking murdered in there," Mel shouted.

He pulled the curtain back. The obese woman had a jagged incision starting at her throat and ending at her bloated stomach. Whoever had killed her, surely it wasn't him, had slashed again at her midsection, spilling her guts, which piled next to her like a large dog's excrement.

Mel looked back at the mirror to find his ski mask pulled up, his terrified expression finding no quarter. He glanced down at his hands. A coppery film varnished his fingers.

Sirens. He could hear sirens.

* * *

Priscilla smacked her palm up against the closed-circuit TV next to her ashtray.

"God damn it, Billy, can't you get us one decent connection?" she asked, her cigarette clinging to a front tooth.

She flexed her jaw as she watched Gloria lead Mel into the bedroom. Her stitches felt loose and the wound that extended from her cleft chin to just under her earlobe burned. She was certain that back alley surgeon had left too much space in between each stitch, despite the fact he moved slower and slower each time he pushed the needle through her flayed skin.

The concrete observation room lacked a mirror, but she knew she looked paler than usual. Her curly red hair, hanging haphazardly down her back in a bushy ponytail, provided the only color against the gray walls. She didn't have much for company. Just a clipboard hanging from a crooked nail, a black rotary phone next to the TV, and the H&K P7 strapped to her leg. She inhaled deeply with her lips wrapped around her cigarette, nursing more than the scars from a job gone horribly wrong.

Priscilla begged Billy to come back to work early. She didn't think he'd cave. She was pretty torn up. She knew her thirst for vengeance leaked through her skin like sweat. Not for the last mark, she had been able to finish the job, but for all men everywhere forever. She didn't know what fueled Billy's hard-on for eradicating his own kind and she didn't care. He was an ally for now. Until they won. Until they didn't need him either. Mel should have been a gift assignment. Matricide. Molestation. Forced abortions. Another man built in God's image, walking free to drink and fuck as he pleased. However, she only felt a deep sadness. The more Mels they exterminated, the more that took their places. A never-ending path of fury that led to bitter disappointment in failing to turn the bloody tide.

The door opened behind her. She didn't turn around, just tipped back in her chipped gray folding chair. Priscilla always smelled Dolly before she came into view. She was certain the girl—yes, girl, Billy was finding them younger and younger— hadn't showered since they picked her up off that pig farm in North Carolina.

"Gloria seems to be enjoying that fucking," Dolly said, watching their coworker ride Mel. "She really have to go that far?"

"Looked like he was pretty persistent," Priscilla said. "Smoked that blunt down by half. Shouldn't be long now. I don't know how he's still going, honestly. Must have been awhile. At least with a woman. He was locked up for quite a bit. Anyway, I wouldn't say that she's enjoying it."

"Better get your eyes checked. That woman ain't faking it."

Priscilla's coworkers often remarked on her eyes behind her back. Blue irises that should have drawn you in were instead dull slivers of cracked paint on an off-white canvas. They conveyed a life that had been taken—raped, really—away.

Those eyes had seen a screwdriver in the vacant, dimly lit lot where Priscilla's attacker had dragged her. She was still unclear about why she chose to wait until he was finished to plunge it into his neck. She had kept her hand on the hilt of the tool long after he went limp inside her and his blood drained all over her. She spent hours with his bulk on her, convinced someone would eventually stumble on the scene. Her rapist had chosen his venue wisely, though, because it wasn't until dusk the next day when two hands rolled the dead man off her.

Priscilla, her face streaked with salt and her white SpongeBob T-shirt stained dark as a bruise, saw Billy standing over her. She had long given up being afraid and waited patiently for him to state his business.

"Think you can do it again?" he had asked.

She had surprised herself when she said yes.

Priscilla wasn't her real name, of course. None of the women she worked with used their given names. Everyone was a famous woman in history. Marilyn, Helen, Eve, Barbara, Cleo (Cleopatra too clichéd and on the nose for even Billy to condone). Zsa Zsa had burned alive in a fire she started to give herself a shot at escaping a kill gone bad. Hepburn was pulled out of the river months after disappearing. There weren't too many left from Billy's first-gen crew—Sunshine now the elder stateswoman reportedly still churning through Nazis in Argentina—and names had taken on a Millennial-era flair: JenLaw, Ginsberg, Knope, Hillary, Melania (against strong objections from Billy, who said that one went against everything the mission stood for).

"Easy, girl," Priscilla said through the cigarette smoke. She watched Gloria smash Mel's head repeatedly into the headboard. She instinctively stood, her hand on the gun's grip. Dolly tensed next to her, too new to know the protocol if Gloria finished the job herself.

"I guess I's wrong," Dolly said. "Damn near killing him. But he looks like *he's* enjoying it more now."

The two women exhaled when they saw Gloria dismount Mel and walk out of the room. Mel didn't even appear satisfied, just finished. He smoked from the joint on the nightstand again, leaving the ashes on his chest.

"You okay to do this?" Dolly asked as she flipped through the pages on the clipboard. "Cut up like that? Mel's a tough assignment on a good day. Shit, they don't pay us enough for this."

"Don't tell Billy, but I'd do this for free," Priscilla said, tapping her fingers on the faux-steel desk. "Did they give me the wrong shit? He should be passed out by now."

Mel was still slumped against the headboard, his eyes drowsy but open. The lab guys had pledged to her this was their strongest batch yet, but they'd been trying to get in her pants for months. They'd do just about anything, including putting her life in jeopardy. God knows what would happen if she came back incapacitated and had to spend time unconscious on their operating tables.

"Did you know Officer Elliot Brinkley's on duty?" Dolly asked. "If someone were to call this in, he'd likely be the one to show up. He drinks on the job. Be damn good if you got 'em both."

Priscilla ignored all five feet of Dolly and picked up the phone. She knew this already. She dialed a number and spoke quietly into the receiver.

"Well, now I'm damn sure he's gonna be there," she said, crumpling her cigarette into the ashtray and slamming the phone down.

"Could be a big night for you," Dolly said. "You up for it?"

"How many fucking times you gonna ask me?" Priscilla said. "There, finally, he's down."

She watched Gloria strut back on screen. She started tugging on Mel's limp body to make sure he was really out cold. Priscilla zipped up her uniform, her fingers lingering on the stitching above her right breast. Her code name never meant much until she was about to do her job. It didn't shield her so much as empower her. Success or failure didn't really matter. It was enough that Priscilla existed and could hunt her prey.

"See ya, Dolly," she said. "Wash your damn self, will you?"

She grabbed the clipboard out of her coworker's hand and stalked out of the room.

* * *

Mel dropped the knife. He expected it to clang against the linoleum, but it meekly sank into the pink shag bathmat. Blood puddled over its sharp edges, encasing it in the grim scene.

"Hope you got paper tahwels in this shithole," he said. "You're a fahking mess."

He stumbled back out into the hallway. She had a galley kitchen, taken up largely by a rusted lime-green refrigerator. He cracked open the door, using the fridge's soft light to illuminate the space. He didn't want to turn any more lights on and bring more attention to the place. He found an empty cardboard roll, but no paper towels. No napkins either.

Mel groped his way to the couch. The floor was a minefield of trash: newspapers, condom wrappers, fast food bags. He found the last of the paper towels wadded up inside a bag of cheese curls, stained bright orange, matching the remote control. The television hiccupped, drawing Mel's attention. The grainy station was broadcasting an "I Love Lucy" rerun, the one where Lucy's about to have her baby, and Ricky, along with Fred and Ethel, trip over themselves trying to get her out the door.

"Hey, wait for me!" Lucy said, watching her husband and best friends bolt from the apartment.

"You said it, you crazy broad," Mel said.

He returned to the bathroom. The crime scene. Not his crime scene, he was sure. He got fucked and then smoked a little grass. Not the recipe for murdering a hooker. If he'd done a line, maybe. Drugs of all kinds made him sleepy though, and he could barely get his dick up for a two-buck whore after a few beers. No, a disgruntled John must have broken in and done it while he was conked out. The worst he could be accused of was rotten luck and a poor choice in billable sex.

Mel opened the door with his boot. He tiptoed around the stagnant puddles of blood and squatted in front of the cabinet under the sink. He fished the knife out of the bodily fluid and used it to pry open the wooden door. The cheap metal lock broke easily, allowing Mel to root through his murdered concubine's bathroom belongings. His hands uncovered a small box of what he was hoping would be tissues. As he pulled it into the light, he saw it was empty save for one last maxi pad. He glanced at the blood and vomit brushed across the toilet seat and back at the feminine product in his hand. He shouldn't have thought of his mother at this moment, but, sure as shit, that's what happened.

Mel was ten years old again, sitting in the convenience store parking lot with Momma's muumuu-clad girth taking up much of the space in the small Volkswagen Bug. She never asked him to go in right away. She would sit in the car, watch all the people driving up and walking through the automatic doors. They had winters, but Mel always remembered it being hot, the sweat stains under her armpits yellowed and growing. Maybe they were just always there.

Funny, he thought. *Momma had no shame when it came to beating us around the house, but plenty when she got out in the world.*

She tamped out cigarette after cigarette into the car's overcrowded ashtray until she found the courage to order him into the store.

"What the fuck you doing sittin' here?" she asked. "Go git mah shit."

Mel would sigh and try not to slam the door in frustration. He'd get a whupping for that.

It was the same order every time. A box of maxi pads and three nips of Old Grand Dad. The cashier knew the kid and never gave him any trouble buying the booze. Whenever the local sheriff happened to loiter in the store, Mel would simply wait him out by reading a comic book he would never buy. He would have loved to peruse a *Playboy* or *Penthouse*, but he would have to break into the plastic wrapping. It was at this point in his life that he felt bad breaking or ruining crap he wouldn't or couldn't pay for.

The cashier, a bright-eyed college student sporting bright green hair, would wink at him somewhat suggestively whenever he'd bring his embarrassing items to the counter.

"You must be a real bleeder," she would say, double bagging everything in obsidian plastic bags.

She'd always throw in a pack of bubble gum or a lollypop just for him. *Momma will end up eatin' it*, he'd thought.

"Don't tell nobody," she'd say, putting her finger to her lips, which were always smothered in purple lipstick. She said the same thing when he stuck her with the knife all those years ago.

He'd nod, wondering what she would look like in a dirty magazine and trying to hide his hard-on behind the counter. Momma never thanked him when he got back to the car. She'd finish smoking her cigarettes, throw the empty pack out the window, curse his father, and then drive off. Mel had never bumped off a convenience store, always thinking he'd run into that cashier again, and maybe she'd end up dead.

Dead, he thought. *That's as good a word as any.*

The sirens had stopped. They were replaced with heavy footfalls on the steps outside. The buzzer inside the apartment rang. Mel found himself walking back to the living room. He pressed a button on the far wall, allowing his fate to walk in the front door without a fight. He snapped to his senses long enough to wrap the knife in the last shred of paper towel and shoved it back into the remaining cheese curls.

"Open up, police!"

Mel did as he was told. He simply unlocked the door and bolted back to the bathroom. He used the maxi pad to wipe off the toilet. He sat down and reached out for the woman's graying hand. He held it tight, now freely accepting whatever happened next.

"Is that marijuana I smell in this shithole?" the officer asked from the door.

"What?" Mel asked.

The cop kicked the bathroom door, causing it to splinter down the middle.

"Pot," he said. "Don't lie to me, junkie. Where's the reefer?"

Mel glanced down at the decaying corpse's hand he was holding in his lap.

"You want some?" he asked.

"Very funny, fucker. Do you want some of this?"

The lanky policeman pulled his sidearm out of its holster and pushed it up against the bridge of Mel's nose.

"For dope?" Mel asked, genuinely curious.

"I pull out my gun for all kinds of things. Not your concern. Where is it? Don't make me ask again."

"Okay, you got it," Mel said, dropping the dead woman's hand and putting his own up in surrender. "This way, Officer …"

"Brinkley."

"Like the ice cream place?"

"Just get moving."

"Are you even going to ask me my name? Isn't that police procedure 101?"

"Are you trying to get me to shoot you, numbnuts? Don't matter what your name is. It's going to be Prison Bitch soon enough."

Mel shut up and led Brinkley into the bedroom. He went straight for the ashtray on the nightstand that contained a joint now the size of a dime.

"Ah, the motherlode," Brinkley said, holstering his weapon. "Do you know how much trouble you're in?"

"Not nearly as much as I thought."

"I didn't buy tickets to a show, so quit the fucking comedy routine."

Brinkley sniffed the spent joint.

"Was this good?"

"Was before ..."

"Before what?" Brinkley asked, taking a toke.

"Nothing. Just a plumbing issue I'm hoping is resolved," Mel said.

"The prison you're going to land in is going to need a plumber after it shits you out," Brinkley said, inhaling deeper on the next hit.

"Huh?"

"Listen, I'm going to ransack this room, and if I find any more weed, I'm just going to plug you, plant a weapon, and claim you threatened an officer of the law."

"What the fuck?!"

"Nah, relax, I'm joking," Brinkley said. "Get a sense of humor. Better get one quick too, I'm hauling you in."

"What?" Brinkley said. "For a little pot. Come on."

"Ha, no, man, you've got a fucking dead body in the tub. You think I'm an idiot?"

"I didn't say ..."

"Do you! Think! I'm! An! Idiot!" Brinkley shouted, pushing the barrel of his gun into Mel's forehead.

"No," Mel said meekly.

"Then get your ass moving. This place is making me sick."

Brinkley grabbed Mel by the arm and led him out of the apartment. Mel expected to see the officer's squad car waiting on the street, but he just saw thin sheets escaping a half-ripped trash bag and ripped up junk mail pushed around by a breeze he couldn't feel.

"You gonna walk me to jail?" Mel asked.

"I'm parked at the bar down the street," Brinkley said. "Didn't want to block the street for an ass hat like you. My beer's waiting, so let's move it."

Mel stopped cold when he saw Priscilla standing in the street ahead of them. Brinkley hadn't looked up yet and his arm kicked back, his grip anchored on Mel's inert frame.

"I'm. Not. Going. To. Tell. You. Again!" Brinkley shouted, reaching for his gun.

"Hands off, officer," Priscilla said, stepping into a shadow behind a pockmarked lamppost. "I could blow your brains out from here right now if I wanted to. You know no one would miss you. I don't know if you'd miss you."

"The fuck are you?" Brinkley said to the dark figure he could no longer see.

"Elliot Brinkley," Priscilla said. "Lowlife beat cop. Never going to make detective. Married five years. Loyal with his dick for, what, two months? Not very smart about it. Your wife got in touch with us. Almost immediately. Questioned her judgment marrying you, but you got that pension. Money from all those scams. Cash you thought you hid so well. She's been cramming that into a savings account for years. And then there's the money from the sex ring. Shouldn't have started sampling, Elliot. I'm not standing here because of a hurt housewife. Well, I'm really here for that shit bag, but ..."

Brinkley's eyes dimmed, his lids closing slowly. His grip on Mel loosened.

"Son of a bitch, did he take a hit of that joint?" Priscilla asked, stepping closer to the two men, but still keeping herself in the dark.

Mel nodded.

"So much for poetry, Brinkley," she said. She aimed her gun quickly and shot Brinkley through the head. Blood and brains rained down over Mel's buzz cut. He shook as Brinkley's body fell.

"Mel, I had a soliloquy planned for you too, but I don't want to waste any more breath tonight. You know what you did, why you did time. I didn't really want to pull this particular job, but we all serve someone, right?"

"You just end a life and cash a check? And I'm the monster?" Mel asked, his voice croaking. "You're just as fahking bad as he is."

"Hun, you're giving me way too much credit," Priscilla said, lighting a cigarette. "I'm just the exterminator."

She took one puff of the cigarette and flicked it toward Mel. It hit him between the eyes right before the bullet did.

"Evenin', boys," Priscilla said, stepping over the bodies. She lengthened her strides as she walked back to the apartment, avoiding the blood now irrigating through the cracks in the cobblestones. Brinkley had left all the doors open. "Nothing like a clean crime scene, officer," she said, shaking her head.

Priscilla marched in, turning more lights on as she made her way to the bathroom. The set designers had outdone themselves this time.

"Glinda, you all right?" she shouted, noticing fake blood footprints in the hallway.

"Bedroom!"

Glinda's feet were propped up on a few pillows, her makeup staining the bed dark maroon. She had her hand in a bag of ruffled potato chips.

"Glad they made up this scene thinking I lived like a pig," Glinda said. "Such attention to detail. Right down to the snacks. I was starving. What took you so long?"

"Brinkley muddied things a bit. Had to get clearance."

"Bet that didn't take long. Piece of shit. I still almost drowned in that fake blood. That would have been something."

"Wagon is on its way," Priscilla said. "Lot of clean up out there, never mind in here. Wouldn't be surprised if they burned down the neighborhood."

"Ain't no one would miss it, neither. Let's roll, baby. We can down a few beers after we punch out."

"Almost made the job easy, Glinda."

Glinda glared at Priscilla for a moment. She slowly took her hand out of the bag and slipped it under the bed sheet.

"That going to be a problem?" she asked.

"Not from me. They'll note it though. May end up in a bloody tub a few more times before you cycle out."

"Just another step on the way to a pine box. Let's go."

Priscilla stepped into the living room and unzipped her coveralls. She crumpled the bulky, itchy fabric into a ball, tossed it on the garbage pile, and then adjusted her form-fitting green dress. The sparkles flickered coldly under the apartment's subpar lighting. Priscilla took a pair of stilettos from the shoe rack near the door and stepped into them. She latched the clasp around her ankle and shook out her long red hair. She couldn't do anything about her scar, but she hoped her curves prevented any man from reading her face.

Glinda waddled up behind her, now dressed in a dark black hoodie and faded out blue jeans. She also couldn't do much with the fake bloodstains on her face, but she had a nondescript baseball cap pulled down as far as it could go.

"Next time, you're the damn cabbie," Glinda said. "They think I don't have hot dresses like that?"

Priscilla didn't answer, eager to get into the car that was surely waiting for them outside. She let Glinda go first. Priscilla took one last look around, including scoping out the wrench Glinda had hidden under the covers, and followed her coworker out the door. Glinda sat glumly in the front seat of a boxy Honda, her face barely visible in the glow of the Lyft dashboard light. A dark van idled at Priscilla's abandoned pile of human flesh, its engine ticking as it cooled. She dropped into the Honda's back seat and heard her dress tear, her legs not used to maneuvering in such tight quarters.

"They gonna charge you for that," Glinda said.

"See, doesn't always pay to be the pretty girl," Priscilla said.

"It always does, sister," Glinda said. "Bet your ass it does."

Ashes

Frenchville, Maine, 1960s

Arthur eased into his rocking chair.

He knew his movements would be limited given the early hour, but his French-Canadian blood didn't allow him to stay stationary while sitting down. He didn't want to wake his wife or young ones, whom he knew wouldn't be up for another hour or so. At least, he hoped those were the only people still asleep in his house. Two of his older sons better be down at the potato farm getting ready for a hard day's work. If they weren't, hellfire would pale in comparison to what Arthur was prepared to unleash.

He took a red box of Winstons out of his front shirt pocket. He slowly and quietly lifted the closest window and the screen behind it. The chill of early October whistled into the house.

Arthur scowled.

He didn't want the first noise of the morning to arouse suspicion. He tapped a cigarette on his wrist and brought it to lips. His first drag was slow and exhilarating, like always. He couldn't help himself from rocking back and forth completely. The old wood floor beneath him creaked.

He sighed, knowing he was sure to hear it from his wife now. He sat still as a hickory switch and waited for her to thunder down the stairs and point an accusatory finger his way. She always preferred catching him in the act rather than grumble about circumstantial evidence, but the moment of crisis passed silently.

Arthur gripped his cigarette with his lips as he straightened his black tie. As the head of the farmhands, he had to look professional. It didn't matter that by the end of the day his white, starched shirt was as dark as his tie. The men respected that he brought class to the job and could still get dirty like the rest of them. He pulled the cigarette away for a moment and watched a clump of ashes fall to the floor. He'd have to remember to sweep them under the radiator before he left.

He felt around his front pants pocket. He angled past his tangle of keys and removed his pocket watch. It wouldn't be long now before Al pulled into his driveway. Arthur risked one more ride in his chair before finishing his smoke. The floor didn't creak this time. His house was on his side for once. He took one last deep, satisfying, soul-enhancing puff and tossed the stub out the window. He stealthily closed the screen and the window. He made sure the rocking chair was at a standstill before rising. He then walked the short distance to the kitchen.

He put the coffee pot on the burner and waited. He had his thermos ready. His sandwich and apple were in a sack in the refrigerator. A turkey sandwich and a Granny Smith was all Arthur needed to get through a day during harvest time. In the off-season, he usually just had the apple. The faint smell of baked goods invaded his nostrils. His wife didn't like when he overdid it on sweets, but she kept making them. He'd find them tonight. Steam rose from the pot and he heard bubbling. He waited another heartbeat before filling up his travel mug.

Al hadn't shown up yet, so his first taste of coffee happened at his kitchen counter. It mingled pleasantly with the tobacco still lingering in his mouth. His eyes rose toward the ceiling as he heard his wife get out of bed. He didn't blink until he heard the bathroom door close.

Arthur sprang into action. He marched back to his rocking chair. He removed his hat from the stand nearby and swept his forgotten ashes under the radiator. He pulled his hand away in pain as the flesh on his right hand contacted the hot metal. He put his hat on his head and again looked toward the second level of the house. He sure wasn't the one that turned the heat on this early in the fall. His wife could have every blanket she owned on her and she'd still insist on the house being ninety degrees. Arthur wore short sleeves indoors year-round.

The couple normally didn't see each other this early in the day. He was usually out the door well before this hour. Yesterday had been a grueling day of harvest, so he gave his crew an extra half hour of sleep to recover. There were thousands of potatoes to yank from the ground, and he couldn't afford to lose any of his men to exhaustion. Arthur didn't leave anything he could directly control to chance. He was even alternating his sons' shifts to keep them fresh. God help them if they took advantage of him being more generous than his old man ever was.

Al honked his horn. Arthur would have to wait to see his wife later that evening. She was making her way down the stairs as he retrieved his coffee and lunch. He was already in the truck's passenger seat when his wife appeared at the screen door.

"Moitzee!" she screamed. "Avez-vous balayez les cendres maudites sous mon radiateur de nouveau?"

Arthur shrugged.

"She's going to light your clothes on fire in the yard one of these days if you keep smoking in her house," Al said. "A big ol' pile of flaming flannel. Hell, half the neighborhood will show up to keep warm and roast marshmallows. That fire will last so long, the town might cut its heating expenses in half."

Highway 1 was empty. The countryside was a blur. Al liked to drive fast.

"Got some new boys starting today. I know, I know, I'm a soft touch," Al said. "They aren't criminals or anything. Just some good boys helping their families. If they go bad you can throw me out too."

Arthur nodded.

"Weather is going to get cold fast," Al said. "It may not seem that way since it's been balls hot during the day, but my feet just won't keep warm at night. You know I tried to sleep with my slippers on the other day? My goddamn slippers. You figure my feet would have sweated through the yarn, right? Nope. My feet were blocks of ice all night. That means we're going to have a bad winter. But then again, I suppose we haven't seen a good winter in more than five years. The only warm thing that happened during the recent winters was your baby girl Gail. What a peach that kid is. She cried for everyone when she was born that February, but not me. You remember that? She liked me best for a while there. I think her brothers scared the hell out of her for a little bit. You can't blame her. If it weren't for you and your wife raising them right, boy, I don't know."

Signals flashed in front of them.

"Dammit," Al said.

The two couldn't see the logging train yet, but they could hear and feel it. They were stopped just before the tracks that cut through the middle of town.

"We're not five minutes away from where we need to be," Al said. "Good thing I got the boss with me, so I don't get in trouble for being late."

Arthur instinctively checked his pocket watch.

"Now don't get ornery on me," Al said. "We've got more than enough time. Besides, those boys have been working hard the past week. A few more minutes of rest won't lose us anything."

Arthur chose not to disagree with that statement at the present time.

"See, look it wasn't even a full train," Al said. "Not a good sign those loads have gotten smaller and smaller. Plenty of trees out here, but not many people demanding lumber, I suppose. Or maybe I'm just remembering the past years wrong. I can't keep all these harvests straight."

They arrived at the farm, and Arthur rushed out of the truck. He walked into the main barn and took his clipboard off his tidy desk. He didn't linger and went back outside. He watched the men head out to the field. He made a small check mark beside each man's name. He noticed many of the men had been here a while, ignoring his orders to get more rest. He liked that. He liked the sight of his son-in-law Onias even more.

Onias, who was married to his daughter Lucille, gave Arthur a quick wave before continuing his work on the old tractor. He wouldn't have been surprised that Arthur hadn't given him a return reply. The two hadn't talked much since Arthur caught wind of the job offer Onias had from a carpentry company in Connecticut. Arthur knew his oldest son Roland had arranged it, which didn't make him any happier. Half of his family was already in that state, so he wasn't thrilled with the thought of another daughter joining them. Besides, Onias was a good worker and a good card player. Arthur knew how much the brothers and sisters hated being apart. It wouldn't be long before everyone moved down there. He was lucky Bobby and Gail were both young enough to be dependent on him, and his wife hated the thought of moving away from where she was born. They weren't going anywhere without him, that was for damn sure.

Arthur wrote in the names of the two men Al had hired the night before when they arrived and checked them off as well. He starred both so he could remember to keep an eye on them. By the time the last man present made it into the field, only two names remained unchecked. And they were both Blanchettes.

He didn't try to stifle his anger. He wouldn't need any more coffee to get his heart rate up. He was thinking of which son's head he was going to dump the rest of it on whenever they decided to show up. He took his pocket watch out and balanced it on his clipboard. Every time he watched the second hand pass twelve, he felt his blood pressure spike. He knew he was going to be at full boil when his sons were standing in front of him. Arthur's son Clifford practically walked willingly into his open hand. As Clifford recoiled, Arthur grabbed the collar of Jimmy's shirt and pulled his face close.

"A man needs to live his life on time! There's nothing more important in his life! Be ass early, be on the dot, but sure as shit don't be goddamn late! You lose a helluva lot more than time when you're late!"

Arthur pushed Jimmy away and walked a few paces away from the boys. It did nothing to calm his anger. Seeing that Clifford's face was red with frustration and hurt made the pot boil over again.

"I'd send you back to your Momma, but she'd goddamn die of embarrassment and shame at the boys she raised!" Arthur shouted. "You let me down. You disappointed me. You lost my respect. Get your asses to work and goddamn earn it back."

His sons ran by him with their heads down.

"Keep those heads up, goddamn it," Arthur shouted after them. "You break a leg after being late and I'm cutting it off myself and throwing you back to work."

He put his hand up to discourage Al from saying a word. Al ignored him as usual.

"A little harsh don't you think?" Al asked.

Arthur didn't reply.

Cheap

1.

"I need a shot of Jameson and a carton of cigarettes," Dawn said.

A shot glass slammed down in front of her.

"I can handle the whiskey part, ma'am," Alan, the bartender, said. He was already pouring the brown liquor into the glass. "But I don't have cigarettes and even if I did, you haven't been allowed to smoke indoors in, say, ten years."

Dawn downed the shot. Signaled for another. Downed that one. Sighed.

"Fuck you, I could smoke outside."

She already felt her body temperature rise a few degrees.

"It's mighty cold out there."

"Pussy."

"Can I get you something else?"

"Don't be so fucking sensitive. You're the one I like." She offered a wave for an apology. "Scotch. Neat and cheap. I'm a thirsty girl on a budget."

More copper-colored alcohol appeared in front of her.

"I'm going to sip this for a while and pretend that you and the cretins here don't exist. That okay with you?"

"Yes, ma'am."

Dawn put the glass to her nose and took a deep inhale. She closed her eyes. She felt drunker without even taking a sip. She leaned back in her seat and put the glass down on the bar. She wanted the shots to really kick in before she started in on the scotch. Cheap scotch is easier to endure when you're already plastered.

"You know how you wish people you work with would just come right out and tell you how they really feel about you to your face instead of passive-aggressively corporate-slamming you behind your back?"

Alan nodded.

"Well, today they finally did." She put her fingers to her lips as if she had a cigarette. "That was right before they fired me."

Her shot glass was refilled. She downed it.

"I'm assuming I'm not paying for that one."

"No, that's on me."

A nod was as close as she came to a thank you.

"What did you do?"

"Huh?"

Dawn had been distracted by the Johnny Cash song playing. "Folsom Prison Blues." One of her father's favorites. Then again, he claimed every Cash song was his favorite.

"For work." Alan tried to discreetly move her empty shot glass away. "What was your field?"

"Who gives a shit? I don't do it anymore. And I don't want this to become me bitching to a bartender I barely like. I don't need a warm, loving human being. I need you to return that glass back full."

Alan pretended not to hear her. He moved on to another patron.

"Why do people feel the need to define themselves by their jobs?" Dawn was really feeling the whiskey-scotch combination in the pit of her empty stomach. "I mean most people hate what they do. And seriously, if you're not delivering babies, cutting into people, or manufacturing rockets, your job isn't that interesting or important. Why not tell people what you do outside of work instead? Currently, I am a part-time yoga enthusiast that aggressively scrapbooks her cat's life. It beats explaining what I actually do for a living. Which I don't do anymore. Fuck it. I love this song!"

"25 Minutes to Go."

Appropriate.

"I'm breaking the seal, so don't give away my seat."

The walk downstairs to the bathrooms seemed harrowing. Even more so now that "25 Minutes to Go" was approaching its violent end. The poor bastard started swinging as soon as she reached the top step.

Good thing I didn't wear my heels.

She reached the bottom just as Waylon Jennings' "Are You Sure Hank Done It This Way" began thundering upstairs. She was going to have to switch from scotch to PBR if this music kept up.

She strutted down to the farthest stall. She sat on the suspect seat in a drunken heap without building a toilet paper nest.

Fuck it.

She started pissing out the alcohol and the gallon of coffee she had consumed earlier that day. If she was a crier, this would have been the moment to let loose. She was just another laid-off broad, one who had been making seventy cents to her dickhead, meathead, adulterous male counterpart's dollar, crying with her ass pressed up against dirty porcelain.

But she felt nothing. Absolutely nothing. All she wanted was for her steady piss stream to stop so she could go back to lusting after nicotine and bad decisions.

She didn't look in the mirror while she washed her hands. It wasn't because she was ashamed. It was because she was busy looking at her legs. She had been hitting the gym and the yoga studio pretty hard recently. The results were spectacular.

She decided to put her heels back on. She pulled the nude shoes out of her overstuffed bag and let them drop on the tiled floor. She took one foot out of her flat and toed it into the first heel without touching the ground. Her ass was one thing, but there was no way her bare feet were stepping on this urine-stained excuse for a floor.

Her hand went instinctively to her hip as she checked herself out. She reached into her bra and lifted up each tit. She unfastened another top button.

"I need to show this shit off to someone. My cheating bastard of a husband certainly doesn't deserve all this."

2.

Dawn wasn't always so mean.

She was here a lot. She probably had a drinking problem. But she was usually a much happier drunk.

Alan hadn't noticed her much at first. The more you tend bar, the more you learn that it's not as easy to notice the onset of someone becoming a regular as people make it seem. He finally cataloged her booming laugh and big tips into his mental regular card file that also featured the old drunk with the clichéd decades-old drinking problem and unsound advice who always sat right in front of the taps.

But he couldn't recall the exact moment he caught feelings for her. It's Bartending 101. Don't fall in love with a patron or someone you work with. You're better off with a drinking problem or STD. Those things are easier to get rid of than a crush or fantasy that has absolutely zero chance of becoming reality.

Alan supposed it started during one of the rare times she invited her husband for a drink. Jealousy springing from the belief you're the superior male can be a powerful thing. The guy could save puppies from execution or read to sick kids at the hospital, but every time he was in the bar next to his wife he seemed like just another douche stealing oxygen from worthier humans. He never stayed long. He always looked uncomfortable. He never looked at her or touched her. He was uncomfortable in this part of her world that he wasn't privy to on a regular basis. As if all that wasn't enough to hate the son of a bitch, he was a shitty tipper.

Alan cleaned off a pint glass and placed it under a tap. He pulled down the tap and watched golden liquid flood into the glass. At the same time, he picked up a cocktail glass and poured the right mix of alcohol and soda into it. He threw a cherry into the mixture. The patron hadn't asked for it, but he knew who it was for. She'd appreciate the gesture. To the untrained eye, it would have appeared as if the pint glass had almost overflowed. He yanked up the tap at exactly the right moment. He could have done it with his back turned, across the street, or taking a shit in the bathroom. He set both drinks on a tray. A waitress took it soon after. He wiped his hands and tossed his towel over his shoulder. There was nothing left to do but wait for the next patron's thirst to demand satisfaction.

Alan found it unbelievable that he let himself think about her at all. His shift ended and he walked back into his life without a second thought about how much he had served and how much he had made in tips. His base paycheck was enough to get him by, so what did he care about making extra? He went to the grocery store, had dinner, studied for his citizenship exam, and sat in front of the television until he had to do it all over the next day.

That's when her smile would pop into his head. Just after questioning how someone could green-light the latest travesty in reality television without consuming enough Quaaludes and LSD to kill a baby T-Rex and right before debating whether he should jerk off in the shower or in bed (she was usually involved in the latter). He usually ignored the smile until he lost his ability or desire to watch the late-night shows. He'd convince himself to forgo the shower and the self-abuse and just pass out as soon as possible. The quicker he fell asleep, the quicker he could avoid wrestling with things he couldn't have.

But, as always, the bar returned to Alan at the exact moment his dreams should have been starting. He was never behind the long stretch of varnished wood. He was standing right next to her. His hand was on her back. They were enjoying drinks together. They were enjoying a lot of drinks together. She was drunk but in a sexy, flirtatious way. She would be showing off her legs. He wouldn't need an excuse to touch them. He just did. They were as smooth as he imagined. She always suggested they lock themselves in the bathroom. She led the way. She walked in. He followed close behind. It was always up against the door. She couldn't wait. She was always wearing a skirt and no underwear. They didn't know what was louder, her screams for more, the people pounding the door to get in, or their bodies thundering against each other. She always flipped off the line on her way out while he took a piss to clear himself out.

He would usually wake up and furiously jerk off. He came out of his waking dream staring at the ceiling of his small, poorly furnished bedroom.

"Who is this woman?" he often said.

She was ordering another drink.

Duty called.

3.

Two suits were sitting at a table nursing watered-down beer.

Well, really it was three suits, but one was slumped up against the wall, passed out, with an unlit cigarette hanging from his fat mouth. He'd lost his company millions that day, so he had gotten a head start on his shitty beer. Two PBRs and a shot of Jameson and the guy was down. Salmon shirts, questionable/non-existent morals, and the lack of ability to drink real booze were the real problems with corporate America.

The two conscious men were clearly disappointed that the bar wasn't livelier. They had walked in ready for action and only found alcoholism, sticky floors, and a fat lump of a woman with one tit hanging out. Not exactly the kind of environment male bravado can sustain an erection in.

They knew better than to approach the decent-looking woman at the bar drinking with purpose. They had picked up enough of her sharp barbs to stay at a safe distance. They could see an up-and-coming douchebag across the way thinking about making a move.

Better him than us, they said to each other talking only with their eyes.

"Where's all the fucking action, man?" the older one said.

"Cold as balls out," the younger man said.

"You'd think people would flock to the bar. Especially guys who have something to go home to. Escape down here on a cold night to watch a little sports and chase tail? That's my idea of a warm winter's night."

A nod in agreement.

"Want to try something harder?" the older guy asked.

"You mean like Heavy B."

"No, you pussy, like scotch."

"With soda?"

"No, on the rocks. What's wrong with you?"

"I don't like straight alcohol. Fucks with my stomach."

"It fucks with everyone's stomach. We're doing it. We need to wake up."

"You mean wake him up?"

The younger man awkwardly pointed at their comatose companion.

"Would you want to wake up if you'd just been shit-canned?"

"Not the way he went out."

"So fuck him."

Scotches were ordered. Low-end. Lower than low. It lazily pooled around the ice, the color of a faded Miller High Life can. Homeless alcoholics wouldn't touch the rotgut these two were taking deep inhales of.

"Smells so good," the younger man said.

"I agree, this is good shit. Should be for the price we paid."

Five dollars each.

First sip. Fits of coughing. Attempts to look manly. Unsuccessful.

"That will wake you up."

"Are you sure I can't put soda in?"

Disapproving look.

"Fine, fuck, I wish there were more tits in this place. Not like a nudie bar or anything, just nice, round breasts to gawk at. Is that too much to ask for?"

"Said the guy who wants to pussy up his drink."

The older man tried to choke down a bigger swallow of booze.

"All I'm going to say is that it's going to be tough getting laid tonight."

"Just like every night of your life."

"Fuck you."

"When's the last time you were with a woman. An actual woman, not someone on YouPorn."

"Wasn't that long ago."

"So like a year?"

"Probably," the younger man said. He hung his head.

"I had one last week."

"Oh yeah?"

"Yup," the older man said.

"That's all you're going to tell me?"

"Yup."

"Just tell me. There's nothing else to talk about."

"Good point."

The two took another small sip. The ice was rapidly melting. The scotch was so bad that even the presence of more water didn't take away its sinister bite.

"So this girl," the older man said, "is a real beauty. She wasn't a freaking supermodel or anything, but definitely fuckable. Man, she sure looked good in jeans. Top-five ass in my book. Her place has a hot tub. She sat on my lap the whole time we were in it. I had a hard-on the size of … um … well … something big."

The younger man held up his pinky.

"That's the size of your mother's dick."

"The one she fucks your father with?"

"You want to hear more or not?"

"Continue."

Another attempt at drinking scotch. Another failure.

"We get out. She's wrapped in a towel. But only her bottom half. Her bikini top might as well not have been there. I mean the straps were holding on for dear life. And she found every opportunity to bend over or rub up against me. My towel could have housed a small Native American village. We're watching this movie on her couch. Wet. Half-naked. Buzzed from some cheap champagne. Her boobs are flopping on my arm every couple of seconds. I don't even know what we're watching because I'm thinking about nailing her any second."

"Dude, this is making me hard."

"Seriously, too much information."

"I'm just saying it's been a while."

"Fuck, I wish *I* was unconscious. I wouldn't have to listen to you."

"I've heard it all," the third suit said. His voice was raspy and broken. "Please don't fuck me in the ass."

A shared laugh.

"So how was she in bed?"

"I wouldn't know," the older man said.

He held a finger up. Brought the two full scotch glasses back to the bar. Came back with two cans. Might as well have had "BEER" stamped on the side.

"They took the scotches off our tab."

"Cool."

The energy improved once the beers were cracked open. Letting beer go warm was a lot easier than stomaching bad booze.

"So what did you say?" the younger man asked.

"Huh?"

"What did you say to scare her off?"

"I didn't say shit."

"You go limp?"

"Do you want to go limp?"

"Just tell me."

"Her phone rang," the older man said. "I knew she shouldn't have picked it up. She paused too long before going for it. Never a good sign. I should have grabbed her and fucked her then. It was her ex. He was sobbing like ... hmm ... like you after jerking it alone every night. He was begging her to take him back. I knew she was going to say yes even when she was telling him no. She went from mostly naked to mostly clothed in about two minutes. Fifteen minutes after she picked up the phone, I was out. My dick was sore as hell the next morning from rubbing up against the zipper on my jeans on the subway ride home."

"Fuck that noise."

Two beer cans touched in a moment of male solidarity.

"Had the same thing happen to me with the last girl I had the opportunity to get with," the younger man said. "We went on a couple of dates. I figured that was enough to warm her up. She was giving me all the signs she wanted me too. Nope. Ex-boyfriend showed up on one of our dates. Short guy, shaved head. Nothing to him. Made a scene. I said something about him being a psycho. She got mad at me! That was it. Great rack she had."

They didn't speak for a while after that. They half paid attention to the hockey game in progress. They were more interested in the sloppy woman headed back to her seat wearing a pair of "Fuck Me" high heels. If the young shit at the next table was going to make a move, now was the time.

"You two piss and moan about these sluts," the third guy said. "I can't imagine what you're going to be like with frumpy wives."

"Go back to sleep," the older man said.

More silence and beer swilling. The bad beer was going down a hell of a lot easier than the scotch. The younger man brought back four more from the bar in preparation.

"What was her name?"

"Whose name?"

"The girl you were just talking about."

"Couldn't tell you."

"You don't remember her name?"

"You remember every girl's name you get with?"

"For the most part."

"Good for you."

"The way you talked about her, though, you've got to remember her name. You don't forget a bust like that just like that. Especially not one you've seen bobbing around in a hot tub all night while your balls sweat off."

"Lydia."

"No shit. Mine too."

"Yeah?"

"Yup."

"Crazy."

"She live downtown?"

"Yeah."

"Shit man, do you think—?"

"City isn't that small. Lot of people live downtown."

"She was a writer though."

"Fuck."

"Same girl, right?"

"Looks that way."

"Good thing we didn't fuck her!"

"Last name?"

"Thompson," the third guy said.

He was wide awake now. He put on this suit jacket. Straightened his tie. Pulled out a wad of bills and left a bunch of them on the table. Took a look at the four beers in waiting. Put a few more bills down.

"You too?" the other two said.

"Fucked her," he said. He got up. Put on a sweat-stained Yankees hat. "Lousy lay. Her boyfriend was outside the door crying like a little bitch. I told her to scream as loud as she could. It was fucked up, but I didn't give a shit."

"Where are you going now?"

"I'm going to pretend none of this shit happened. See ya fellas."

He left.

5.

A beefy arm landed on the bar.

It slithered to a pint glass overflowing with Magners. The chubby hand attached to the end of the hairy, varicose-veined arm held onto the glass firmly but shook so much the top layer of liquid sloshed over the side and onto the bar.

"Feck. These guys fill it too high," Claudette said. No one was sitting to either side of her. She was alone at the end of the bar, like always. "Next one I'm dumping on their fecking heads."

She wasn't overweight like the rest of her alcoholic brethren. She just had huge tits and a huge ass. And her arms had a little extra cottage cheese. There isn't a law against any of that. She did sit-ups every night after her hard cider dinner to keep her figure where it was. She didn't want to be a complete cliché.

Claudette felt old as shit. Her seventy-fifth birthday was approaching, and all she had to show for it was a ripped piece of paper with a bunch of bad football picks on it. The sports news was coming on soon, so some of those picks might improve. She hoped so, at least, she needed help making rent this month. Disability and Social Security weren't going to cut it this month.

"Your left breast is hanging out," Alan told her.

"And?"

"I thought you might want to put it back in. Some people are trying to keep their drinks down."

"You don't think they appreciate fine titties?"

"Come on, give me a break."

"I was giving my nipple some air, take it easy. Jesus, rough night at the circle-jerk last night?"

Alan shrugged and walked away.

"He's upset because mine was the first tit he'd ever seen. He was saving himself for Scarlet Johansson. Fecking bastard."

The seat next to her was empty. She missed the sports news segment. She was face down on the bar asleep.

"Son, can you help me with these?"

Someone was actually there this time. His skinny, blonde girlfriend too.

"We're having a conversation here," the girl said.

"Well, we're about to have one too," Claudette said. "Funny, because I bet both involved a woman taking money from a guy."

"Excuse me?!"

"You're a whore. I thought it was clear. Maybe my joke wasn't that good."

"What can I help you with?" the guy asked. He wanted to avoid a scene, mainly because his girlfriend was a whore. He didn't need the cops becoming involved in an already unpleasant situation.

"Giants or Eagles?"

"Eagles."

Claudette circled "Giants" on her paper.

"Patriots or Browns?"

"Patriots."

She looked down at her paper. Then back at him. Held his eyes for a moment.

"Patriots it is."

It went like this until she was done with that week's slate of games.

"Thanks. You shouldn't let her overcharge you. I've seen her in here before. Looks like a bum lay to me."

She took a deep pull from her Magners and ignored the girl's ranting.

"Who are you talking to today?" Alan asked, no longer able to ignore Claudette talking to empty air.

The young man wasn't there. He had been, though. Claudette was sure of it.

"Feck."

"A guy named Fuck?"

"No," she said. "Cunt. C-u-n-t. Cunt. Like your mother."

"My mother spelled it with a K."

"Christ, I've got other customers. Keep the crazy in check."

6.

Dawn took another shot of Jameson. Just another drink closer to forgetting her cursed life.

"Excuse me, are you talking to me?"

A young man was standing next to her waiting for Alan. She could tell by his blue shirt and tan pants he was about to order a light beer or harmless mixed drink.

Alan showed up before she could answer him.

"Can I get a gin and tonic?"

Bingo.

"I don't fuck my husband, what makes you think I'd be interested in fucking you?"

"I'm sorry?" The young man, a child really, asked.

"Son, I'd be able to sense the erection you're harboring in your khakis if I was standing at the edge of the city during a hurricane." She applied more red lipstick. "I know for a fact the cheap sluts in this dump aren't giving you a rise."

Alan handed the young man a drink. Waved off his money. Gave him a look of apology. Poured Dawn another shot.

"Can you start being nice so I don't have to kick you out?"

"Can I give you a $100 tip so you can go back to not giving a fuck?"

"Just try not to piss off some of the other people here who might want to leave me a big tip."

"Aye, aye, Cap'n."

She stood up and saluted him sloppily.

Back to modern music. She didn't know the song or the artist. Yet she found herself humming along to the chorus. That's how you knew they created this shit in a lab, she thought. It gets to you whether you want it to or not.

"I saw a fat guy dressed up in a bear costume playing the key-tar on a subway platform on my way over here," she said. "What happened to high subway performance art?"

"Wow, you look amazing for someone that just got fired."

A female coworker who Dawn was convinced gobbled enough corporate cocks to choke the engine of a C-5 sat down on the stool next to her.

"Do you think we're going to bond now?"

"I'd had a feeling you'd be here."

"Good for you."

"Can I buy you a drink?"

"No."

"I'm going to buy you a drink."

No doesn't mean no anymore, apparently. It's just a way to start a negotiation only one side wants or cares about. Bad enough she had to listen to those pigs talking about their conquest of the same woman. Took a lot for her not to smash a bottle over their heads.

A thin man who had just arrived at the bar diverted her attention.

He was short. His skin was light brown. He was clean-shaven.

"Bud Light."

His accent pegged him as Indian.

Dawn didn't know why she was fascinated with him. He was unremarkable. Another banker. Another empty suit. Someone on a higher rung than she was.

Her coworker—ahem, ex-coworker—was saying something about personal accountability and professionalism. Something else about galvanizing someone's balls.

This guy was really chugging his beer. She shivered thinking about how all that Bud Light tasted at once.

"Regular Budweiser, please."

"I'll get this one," Dawn said.

The man thanked her tersely. Pounded that beer. Paid for his first one. And left.

"Why did you buy him a drink?"

"That was some brilliant drinking. He chased a shitty light beer with a shittier heavy beer in the time it takes me to take a sip of scotch. Inspired drinking needs a reward."

"Did you hear anything I just said?"

"No."

"No?"

Struggling with the concept again.

"Do you want me to repeat it?"

"You know what bars are for, right?"

"Yes, but I don't spend as much time in them as you do."

A pulse!

"They fired me the day they hired me. There's nothing else to say."

"You had so much po—"

"Stop. I had the ability to take bullets for conflict-averse higher ups so crippled with indecision it probably takes them an hour to figure out what stall to take a shit in. That's not potential. That's—I don't know what it is, but it's far from potential."

"What are you going to do now?"

"Do you care?"

"Yes."

"Why?"

"I like you."

"Sexually?"

"You're not my type. I like your passion."

Sass!

"That's the other thing that got me canned. Made them a ton of money making them and everyone else uncomfortable. You're welcome."

She raised her glass. The bartender thought she needed a refill. Poured another glass. Slid it in front of her.

"That's what I'm going to do next."

"What?"

"Get men to give me drinks that fast."

7.

That didn't go well.

Glen hadn't expected her to be that icy and dismissive. The recently canned woman, who had dismissed him out of hand for his obvious erection, was now feeding dollar bills into the jukebox. He saw his credits adding up. He started selecting country songs at random. Cash, George Strait, George Jones, Alan Jackson. Names he vaguely remembered from his days listening to his mother's small radio in her small kitchen in the family's small house.

He didn't do anything small anymore. Big music played out of a big stereo system in a big apartment overlooking a big city.

The woman was right. He had a hard-on. One that couldn't be ignored.

Glen had been wearing it since she walked in the door. He had been pretending to care about his coworkers' gossiping. In his mind, no one's life was more interesting than his own. He humored them and added his presence to their outings merely to keep up appearances. You couldn't keep getting ahead if no one knew who you were or thought you weren't a sociable "team player."

Usually, he didn't find a whole lot of talent in the dive bars they insisted on going to. They were all wealthy but slumming in these places had become somewhat of a tiring addiction. He knew how the other half lived and didn't need a refresher every Friday afternoon.

His cohorts had already started leaving in dribs and drabs by the time this woman strode in on a gust of electrified estrogen and sexy indifference. He was completely alone now by the neon jukebox, awkwardly trying to push his dick into an uptuck.

Glen had one goal his whole life: Get money.

Money was the key to ditching his backward family. Money was how he signed the lease to his swank address. Money was the reason he never went hungry in a city known for making people whine about buying ramen noodles and cheap canned beer on their blogs.

He had taken care of his bank account in short order. Law school, law firm, rapid rise, corporate lawyer. Promotions, golf club memberships, bonuses, tax evasions, suspect investments with monster payoffs, and a small inheritance when his useless parents finally kicked.

Now he had a new goal: Get pussy.

Not that it took much effort, thanks to the money. It opened a lot of legs. "No" was not something he heard often.

"I don't fuck my husband, what makes you think I'd be interested in fucking you?"

His face reddened.

Glen was determined to have sex with her tonight. He sensed she wanted it. Why mention the husband and fucking if you didn't want something to happen? It was as much a game to her as it was to him.

He kept adding songs to the jukebox. Acted like he was really studying his choices. Each new song prompted her to moisten her panties. She loved each one. He inserted more money into the machine. He was going to fill her with as much steel guitar as possible before filling her mouth up.

"Love me some Brooks & Dunn!" she screamed at the bar.

Only a matter of time.

8.

Motherfucker.

Dawn left her scarf on the stool.

Shit.

Alan stopped wiping up the scotch that had sloshed out of her glass all night and reached over the bar to grab it. He held it in his hands. It was silk. He was sure it smelled just like her—a mix of Dove soap, booze, aggression, and a bitchy cold streak.

He looked toward the door she had just exited. His eyes then focused on the debauchery she left behind. He didn't want to give a fuck about a stupid scarf. She probably had hundreds of them. She was so drunk she probably wouldn't even remember she had worn one today.

Then again, if he rushed out, handed it to her, she might remember him a little more fondly the next time. She could even say thank you. Or invite him into her cab.

He could also just wrap the thing around his dick tonight. That seemed like the best option at the moment.

Out of the corner of his eye, he spotted the young asshole that had tried to hit on her earlier settling up with the other bartender. He recognized the look in the guy's eyes. The prick kept glancing out the main window to make sure she hadn't left the sidewalk yet. The bartender's heart jumped as he saw a cab pull up.

Some pricks finish last, shithead.

And sometimes you're the prick, his mind fired back.

9.

Dawn stood drunk at the edge of the sidewalk.

She raised her hand in the air. A taxi promptly parked in front of her. She gave the driver the finger. The guy started shouting and honking his horn. She kicked the side of his passenger side door.

"Fuck off! I don't fucking need you."

The cab drove off. She still needed a ride home, but she wanted the world to know she was still in control. She decided what happened in her life.

She noticed the cold for the first time.

Fucking polar vortex. Still hanging on in mid-May. The fuck.

She really needed a smoke. It had been too long. She had quit for, what was it, two weeks now?

She felt that would gain her at least a couple of weeks on the backend.

10.

Alan stopped Glen at the door. He angrily threw her scarf into the middle of his chest.

"Give this to that crazy bitch out there if you run into her," he said. The guy looked like he was nursing the worst erection in recorded history. He noticed a pack of Marlboro Reds in his pocket and salivated in his mind. "And tell her she's not welcome here anymore. My boss is pissed."

Glen nodded.

Alan knew he wouldn't actually tell her any of that. The damn kid probably wouldn't remember it until after he's emptied his balls.

He looked at her one more time. She was cold. Drunk. Hurt. About to make the kind of decisions one does when cold, drunk, and hurt.

A customer asked him for a drink. Rudely.

Alan turned back to his work. He knew he was going to let her right back in the next time.

I really should have kept that scarf for tonight.

11.

Dawn put her hand up again.

All the taxis that drove by her were occupied. The light turned red on Second Avenue. She could see a vacant cab idling. She waited impatiently. She took the lighter out of her pocket and flicked it off and on. She really wanted a cigarette.

"Need one of these?"

A pack of Marlboro Reds appeared near her elbow.

"Are you trying to give me cancer tonight?" She put her hand sloppily on her hip. "Why not just offer me heroin next time."

"You want one or not?"

She eagerly snatched one out of the pack. She shoved it in between her lips and quickly lit the end of it. She sucked in deeply. She vowed never to suck anything as deeply as she was sucking this unfiltered cigarette. She looked at Glen. He seemed more handsome under a dimly lit streetlight and a half a bottle of cheap booze.

Hold that thought.

A taxi pulled up to the sidewalk.

"You want to have a good time tonight, junior?"

Glen nodded.

She held the door open for him as he climbed in the back seat. She smiled for the first time that night.

"Pussy."

Go Maire Sibh Bhur Saol Nua

"Did you have a nice day, dear?"

It took Sarah a moment to realize the petite Irishwoman seated next to her on the DART was talking to her.

"Um, yes! I mean, sure. Huh?" she said, kicking her slumbering fiancé Dylan in the shins.

"Ow!" he said.

His crumpled map flew off his lap. The stranger picked it up, smoothed the thin paper, and folded it neatly along the worn creases. She handed it back to Dylan, whose New York City sensibilities snatched it cautiously. The woman either didn't register or ignored his apprehension. She adjusted her horn-rimmed glasses and continued to smile.

"I'm sorry, what were you saying?" Dylan asked.

"Have you two enjoyed your day so far?"

Sarah and Dylan eyed each other before offering their new traveling companion a smirk and a shrug.

"We got engaged in London!" Sarah blurted out.

"I'd be surprised if you haven't heard yet," Dylan said. "She told every cab driver, waitress, and bartender between London and Dublin."

"There's an ocean between them, dummy," Sarah said, sticking her tongue out.

"Oh!" the woman exclaimed, oblivious to their banter. "My word. That's the best news I've heard all week. Magical. Let's see that ring!"

Sarah presented her left hand like a starlet mugging for the camera on the red carpet. Knuckles and fingers collided as the woman examined the sparkle.

"Marvelous," she said. "Matches your complexion perfectly. Nicely done, young man. Couldn't be happier for you two. Love it. Unless he's a lout, dear, but by the looks of him, I'd say he's a gentleman."

"My mother might say otherwise, but I try," Dylan said. "What's your name?"

"It's Madeline," she said. "But you don't have to trouble yourself with that mouthful. Maddy works just fine."

"Dylan," he said. "That's Sarah."

Maddy delicately shook Sarah's ring hand, still entranced by the ring's diamond halo and rose gold band.

"Tell me everything," Maddy said. "How'd you two meet?"

"Job interview," Dylan said. "She applied to be my assistant. She ended up on the fast track to wife. Go getter."

"Hush," Sarah said. "I deflected your advances for a good long while. Took him weeks to summon the gumption he needed to ask me out in person. Who sends a direct Twitter message? Really Dylan, it would have been so easy to say no."

"You intimidated me," he said.

"I'm real sorry," Sarah said, motioning to her slender figure. "What was so scary? Was it my pastel summer dresses or the pink cupcakes I made the office on Valentine's Day that frightened you so?"

"I rest my case," Dylan said. "Maddy, we haven't asked about your day. How was it?"

"I've been up and at 'em since five a.m.!" she said. "Met up with some friends in the countryside and we hiked some hearty Irish trails. Probably six miles all told! I'm hungry, achy, and exhilarated, but not necessarily in that order."

Maddy showed off her muddy hiking pants by swinging her short legs, which barely allowed her feet to touch the train's floor. Her thin face burned fuchsia as she coaxed a last drop of water from her emerald Nalgene bottle.

"Considering how much beer and Guinness stew I've had the last couple of days, I may need to hike straight across the country," Dylan said, patting his thickening midsection. "And I'm not even counting the whiskey!"

"I'm guessing you're making plenty of friends at the pub," Maddy said. "Especially considering your lovely, golden-haired fiancée."

"Bus drivers, rambunctious sons, folk singers, you name it," Dylan said. "There was a lot of pining wherever we went."

"Everyone has been so friendly," Sarah said, dismissing Dylan's commentary with a wave of her hand. "Refreshing change of pace from back home."

"Some of us may not have much in Dublin, but we're usually good for a decent conversation and a pint!" Maddy said. "How'd he propose, dear?"

"We were in St. James Park in London and I decided to walk a few feet away to get a picture with Big Ben in the background—"

"Yeah, first thing she says to me as I walk up to her is, 'You could have waited by the bench; I was coming right back,'" Dylan interrupted. "Tough cookie."

"You love it," Sarah said. "He started getting all poetic, which isn't out of the ordinary for a writer like him, and I figured he was just caught up in the excitement of his first trip abroad. He said something about the beginning of our next adventure and I realized what was happening. And down on his knee he went!"

Dylan stood and bowed dramatically. Maddy laughed and applauded.

He dropped back into his seat as the train stopped abruptly. The conductor announced the station, which caused Maddy to slap herself on the forehead.

"I've overshot home by two stops!" she said. "Talk about getting wrapped up in the drama!"

"Oh, sorry about that," Dylan said. "Is it a pain to catch one going the other way?"

"I'll just grab a taxi at the next stop. Or add a couple more miles to the day's total. Your folks must be thrilled with all this good news."

"Well, I'm sure mine would be if we could get them on the phone," Sarah said. "We've only gotten in touch with my grandmother. She was in the bathroom at the casino. She said, 'I don't need to worry about losing here because I just won a million dollars.' That's going to be a tough quote to top."

"My folks are thrilled," Dylan said. "I think they had given up on me finding the right woman some time during George W. Bush's first term. I know my niece Elizabeth will be excited. She called Sarah a keeper the first time she met her. That was well before Sarah decided that she liked me."

"I'm sure she knew well before that," Maddy said. "It was the blue eyes and dark hair, right?"

Sarah blushed and nodded.

"He also has a way with words," she said. "You'd think because I'm a writer myself that I'd be immune to his charms, but I just melt."

"That's because I save my best words for you," Dylan said.

"Aw," Sarah said. "You better."

"That's as good a note to end on as any," Maddy said. "I can't miss another stop!"

The train had slowed to a crawl as it neared the next station. Other travelers shuffled past them and lingered around the nearby vestibule.

"Sorry again," Dylan said. "And sorry about being weird when you started talking to us. Like Sarah said, we're more used to people soliciting us for money on the subway."

"It's quite all right, dear. *Go maire sibh bhur saol nua*," Maddy said as she stood. "That means, 'May you enjoy your new life.' You two are going to love every minute of it."

Her eyes welled with tears, allowing Dylan and Sarah to glimpse a deep pain that had previously been masked by the woman's relentless cheerfulness.

"Thank you," Sarah said, grabbing Maddy's hand. "We're happy we got to share our story with you."

"Agreed," Dylan said. "Get some rest once you finally land home."

"Oh, I'm too revved up to sleep now!" Maddy said, once again slipping behind her optimistic veil. "Hang on to each other forever, loves."

The train stopped and the conductor bellowed, "Dun Laoghaire." The doors opened with a satisfying *pop!* Maddy hesitated for a moment and then blew Dylan and Sarah a kiss. She hopped off the train just as the doors were about to close.

Dylan collected the day's souvenirs scattered next to him and plopped down in Maddy's abandoned seat next to Sarah. He gripped his fiancée's hand as she admired her new treasure for the thousandth time. Sarah elbowed him lovingly after catching his eye roll. He smiled as he closed his eyes and fell asleep.

Waiting

1.

Chet cracked an egg against a stainless-steel mixing bowl. He caught the egg white in the broken pieces, letting the yolk spill out and ooze down his tanned, cracked hands. He dumped the clear liquid into the bowl and repeated the process with five more large brown eggs. He spooned in a dollop of soupy sour cream, which blobbed inertly in the egg whites' puddle. The clang of the utensil against the bowl echoed in the otherwise empty kitchen as he forced the remaining cream into the mixture. The lone feathers tattooed on each of his forearms flexed as if in flight while he beat the eggs and sour cream together.

It was a culinary trick Chet learned from his father. Every fifth omelet or so you served to a customer, hit them with sour cream instead of milk or half and half. Chet even went so far as to drop in the smallest amount of vanilla or bourbon possible— just enough of something alien so that the diner questioned whether or not it was ever really there. Every time, the wait staff never failed to tell Chet, "Oh, man, they went bonkers for that omelet. What did you put in there, bro?" The person's next run of morning meals would still be deliciously average. Never transcendent, never special. Until that fifth or so time rolled around and their palette was greeted with something it didn't even remember missing. What Chet could do with breakfast food.

A seven-year-old August pushed through the kitchen door just as his father lit a burner on the stove and poured the milky substance into a pan. Chet's son, short for his age, didn't quite rise above the countertop, so Chet didn't notice him until he had wrapped his arms around Chet's leg.

"Yo, kid, if I fall and break your melon like these eggs, it's on you," Chet said. "What you got in your mitt?"

"You told me to get to work, so I did!" August said, holding up a piece of tan construction paper. "It's you!"

"Hey, look at that," Chet said, examining the scene August had drawn while pushing the egg whites around in the pan. "You didn't make my ass look too big, thanks son. Don't be sayin' *ass*."

"I want to be a cook just like you when I grow up," August said, taking the paper back and admiring his own work.

"No, you aren't. I'm not sweatin' over here so you can end up sweatin' next to me. Or sharpening my knives or whatever else I would make you do for killin' my dream. You got to be a lawyer or some shit. Stuff. Don't be sayin' *shit*. That way I can watch you bust your hump and I can make pictures of you. How's that sound?"

"Sure. But you'll still make me eggs, right?"

Chet fell into a fit of laughing.

"Yeah, I'll make you eggs. You always get sour cream. Now get back to the bar before Ruby catches you in here. She'll be red hot from the bank."

"Too late," Ruby said, walking in the side door. "And she is sure as shit red hot."

"Don't be sayin' *shit*, Ruby," August said.

Chet shrugged at Ruby while dumping diced peppers, onions, and shredded cheese onto a fluffy, eggy mattress.

"A. Gust, why don't you go back inside and print me some money."

He did as he was told. He ran back into the restaurant and danced over to his stool in the far-left corner of the bar. He pawed through his sheaf of construction paper and pulled out a bright green sheet. August studied it for a moment, ultimately deciding it wasn't the precise shade he was looking for. Plus, the construction paper was too wimpy. This job called for a clean white sheet of oak tag and Asparagus from his 200-count Crayola crayons bucket. He reached over the lemons, limes, and cherries and pulled a black spill mat shouting the name of some artisanal vodka back with him. It was a little sticky, but since he forgot his ruler this would have to do. He sharpened the crayon—which made him hungry for his father's pea soup every time he used it—and slowly traced out a perfect rectangle using the mat's edges.

August eyed the sole waitress on duty and her handful of customers. He needed a little recon for his next steps. He slid three stools down and quickly grabbed a folded bill in the tip jar. He was relieved to discover it was just $1. Whenever he happened to pluck out a $10 or $20—to confirm which president was on it or use as a straight edge—the bartender would snatch it back in an instant. But no one would miss a single for the short amount of time he would use it.

Returning to his seat, August first sketched out George Washington's face and drew a circle around it with his loosely closed fist. He retraced his markings with the crayon, then lightly erased the pencil marks when he was done. His exactness typically never made it much further. He was too eager to see the final product to worry about having all the details completely right. However, a command from Ruby always warranted extra effort. He carefully wrote out "$100" in each corner. He skipped the boring parts of money, including legal jargon and serial numbers, and shaded in the whole rectangle with his crayon. The color seemed a little off to him, so August added a light touch of canary-yellow where the white paper showed through the green.

"Good start, August," he told himself.

August. Even at that age, his name confused him. He assumed his mother—whoever she was—had gifted it to him before she went wherever absent parents go. August was certain that Chet's composition lacked even a single stanza of poetry. His father resembled a brawny, six-foot wrecking ball, one that came home weepy and drunk when he cooked the late-night shift. August would run his hands through Chet's shaggy brown hair and hold a cool cloth to his forehead whenever the man collapsed in the king-sized mattress on the floor in the master bedroom. Chet had yet to acknowledge it or thank him.

August imagined his mother as a fair-skinned poet on some never-ending literary tour. She must have been someone with enough imagination to believe he'd grow into a name reserved for gladiators or statesmen. Living up to it seemed a burden at times, but because August was sure she gave it to him for a reason, he kept the small ambitious flame inside him burning even when all he wanted to do was play video games or wrestle with his father.

Here's where his monetary minting plan got tricky. He had to ignore an unbreakable rule to complete his mission. It's not like August didn't enjoy tiptoeing around Ruby's strict edicts, but he knew he wasn't allowed by her table by the window under any circumstances, and absolutely, no-way-no-how, beware-the-penalty-of-death, could he even think about using her shears. A couple entered the restaurant, giving him just enough cover to sneak over and cut out his newly minted hundo. August quietly placed the scissors down where he found them and hustled back to the bar. He considered his creation, tilting his head left and right, trying to identify any glaring little kid mistakes. He made a few adjustments with his green and yellow crayons, but his attention span finally ran out. It was time to share. Maybe this would help Ruby.

August had his hand on the kitchen door, but the one-sided shouting stopped him from pushing through to the other side. He just crouched and listened.

"... no pretending to clack away at his keyboard," Ruby said. "No consulting his boss in some back room. Just, 'no.' His eyelids didn't even flutter. 'No.' A plain no. Like this place ain't been open for five years doing good business. Like people don't think we're part of the neighborhood. Like that lovely reporter didn't profile us in the *Queens Tribune*. 'No,' he says. Probably had his mind made up when I made the appointment. Not one more dime from them. There goes any dream I had of expanding. I'll bet you that worm will be here for brunch on Sunday. You watch, he'll sit where I can see him no matter where I am. Rubbing it in my face. I'd like to rub some of that corned beef hash in his face, tell you what. That'll teach them to operate the way they do. The way I talked to him walking out the door, I wouldn't be surprised if he pays off the health inspector to close me down. Get me off the block and off their books at the same time. Don't mean nothing to them."

Chet held out his metal stirring spoon and let it drop on the hard-tiled floor. Ruby jumped but would only let annoyance crease her face.

"You miss the part where I told you Astoria was known for Greek and Eastern European food when you moved in? Soul food doesn't always mix well with gyros and goulash. Black belongs in Harlem. Well, until bankers like him take that over too. Won't even let you have chicken and waffles."

"Gonna lecture me about racism now?" Ruby replied. "And disrespect chicken and waffles on top of it?"

"You love my chicken and waffles."

"Not the point."

"This guy really got to you, huh?" Chet asked, flipping the omelet.

"How can you tell?"

"You're not cursing."

"The fuck you mean?"

"See, you only curse when you're not really upset. Or you're trying to make a point. Or if you're talking to me."

"Yeah, well, you try talking to you without cursing."

"I have. Nothing gets through this thick head but fuck, shit, or cun—."

"That's too crude even for my tastes, baby," Ruby said, putting her hand up to shut Chet up.

"You ticked off because I'm dating Denise?" Chet asked, nodding his head toward the door.

"Don't know what you're implying, but, no," Ruby said. "Other than I'm gonna have to hire some other jailbait tart once you're done sampling this one. She been to your place while August was there?"

"They've become acquainted."

"Hm, helps when they come from the same playground at school. Be careful with that boy. He's sensitive. Losing people ain't the same as losing those goldfish I told you not to bring home."

"So we goin' under or what?" Chet asked, changing the subject. "Can I stop making omelets for these people today so I can start job hunting? Likely gonna take a while, you know what I'm sayin'?"

"Restaurants 'round here will hire a cook with your skills off the street."

"Not one as white as me."

"You go from lecturing me about racism to being racist. That's some shit. You're threatened with a little adversity and it's the black brothers and sisters to blame? Pulling that reverse racism junk on me. Now of all times."

"I'm not mad about it. Just sayin'," Chet replied. "And it's my *hermanos* and *hermanas* keeping demand for costly Americans like me down. Simple math."

"Ain't nothing simple about the math spewing out of that shit hole in your face."

"That what you wore?" Chet asked, waving his whisk in her direction.

"Yeah, the fuck's wrong with it?"

"It's a little ... willowy."

"Oh, so it's better if people who look like me should dress in honky straitjackets with a noose hanging off the back for convenience?"

"So you want them to take you seriously, but you also want to walk around looking like that woman dragging thirty plastic bags filled with rotten fruit on and off the N train at Astoria Boulevard?"

"If that wacko could cook, I'd fire you and hire her right this second. Where'd you learn to be this fucking infuriating? Hope it's not genetic because I actually love your son. Fuck you know about fashion? I know you rock those blue, ripped up Giants sweatpants when I'm not here. Can't even find fucking respectable chef pants. I spend half my day trying not to fucking think about how fucking angry you make me. If I get an ulcer, I'm naming it Fuckin' Chet."

August took Ruby's continued cursing as a sign his presence might be more welcome than it was a couple of minutes ago.

"Your troubles are over, Ruby," he said, holding up his makeshift currency, only now realizing he should have colored in the backside.

"You came back with my money, A. Gust!" Ruby exclaimed.

"I sure as shit did!"

"Hey!" "Yo!" Ruby and Chet said at the same time.

"Stuff! I sure as stuff did!" August replied.

Ruby held the heavy paper up to the light and mumbled something. She eyed August, making him momentarily regret signing up for this job. She signed dramatically.

"Yup, that's the real deal, all right," she said finally. "At least I can count on one of your kin for help. Why don't you go back to the bar and make me ten more of these. I'm gonna need every last one."

"Sure!" August said, assuming he now had implicit permission to use her scissors. And anything else on her table or in the restaurant for that matter.

He worked diligently for another hour, his crayons worn down to inch-long stubs by the time he cut out the last bill. His meticulousness had waned with every fresh piece of paper, his youthful attention span distracted by the cartoons the bartender had turned on to prove his effervescent hipness to the diner. August was alone for that hour, no one wanting to sit and drink next to an elementary school kid. Until, of course, Bernie, Branchhall's mothball-scented regular staggered to the bar and ordered a Bloody Mary and five pieces of bacon. She smiled crookedly at August, letting him know his time in her rightful place was severely limited.

That suited August just fine because he sensed trouble when his father walked out of the kitchen before Ruby did. She never spent more than an argument's worth of time in there. The fact that she wasn't seated at her table eating or drinking and Chet was talking softly to the hostess he had been ordered to treat politely the other night at dinner spelled bad news for the rest of August's day.

It felt like every eye in the restaurant was fixed on that swinging door when Ruby walked through it. She clutched her flowing crimson jacket a little closer to her chest. She set her plate down, which was heavy from the omelet Chet had made her, down on the thickest tablecloth in the place and pulled on the arm of the nearest waiter. She spoke quickly into his ear. The lanky teenager with a mop of brown curls raced to the bar where the bartender stood waiting with a Champagne Mule in a golden flute.

His father's friend—August had been trying and failing to remember her name—took a deep breath and headed over to Ruby. August didn't know what was said or agreed to there because he was watching his anxious father scratch at his feathers like he was allergic to them. Chet blew Ruby a kiss as the young woman, her face scrunched and red, bounced out the front door.

"Bye, Denise!" August yelled after her, finding the right name just before the door closed completely. He glanced toward his father, hoping to be surprised by some show of gratitude for his loyalty and ability to follow directions. Instead, Chet caught the door handle just as the thick wood settled into the door jamb.

"Yo, Ruby, babysit the kid for a few? Running low on dip cans. Need to restock."

"Assuming this will be a quick trip?" Ruby replied.

"Down the street and back. Fifteen minutes," Chet said, taking a look outside, rethinking his answer. "Twenty, tops. I know how busy you are planning Queens domination."

Ruby waved her hand—as close to a blessing as Chet ever got from anyone.

"Remember what we talked about before?" August's father asked him while half in, half out of the oak door.

"Lawyer or some shi—stuff," August said, but thought, *astronaut, actor, Ghostbuster.*

"That's right. Nothing less. You'll never be less, kiddo."

"Sure, Dad, I get it. But hurry up, okay? I want to go home."

"You got it, buddy. Be back in a few. Sit tight."

Chet left and August chose a new duo of freshly sharpened crayons. He'd be working with peach and blue until his father returned. He squiggled a few aimless lines on a nearby place setting but decided he earned a few more minutes of cartoons.

August listened to Ruby's fingers pounding her calculator's keys and waited.

2.

Twenty-five years later, August twitched nervously on his favorite bar stool with no illusions that Chet would ever set foot in his life again. He wouldn't be waiting long this visit, at least according to the new waiter.

"I'm August, by the way," he said, extending his hand.

"I know," the guy said, looking at August's hand like it was a cockroach sulking across the bar. "That's what they told me back there. When I asked when your basket would be out. And then I told you it'd be ready soon."

"And your name?" August asked, pulling his hand back and rubbing the feather on his left arm.

"Hank."

"Well, nice to meet you, Hank. You from Queens or?"

"Bell Boulevard. In grad school over at Queens College. And then headed wherever New York City isn't."

"Solid plan. You look familiar. You work anywhere else I might know?"

"Last job was at T-Bone Diner on Queens Boulevard. Can't escape the boulevards, I guess."

"That's it," August said. "Used to go there all the time. Stayed until closing time more often than not. Got a lot of writing done until midnight hit. What I can do fueled by pie and the end-of-the-night coffee. Seeing that neon sign with the busted "IN" coming out of the 71st/Continental station always felt like home."

"So now you're a regular here?"

"Sort of. That's the easiest way to sum it up. This place actually *is* home."

"Sure," Hank said. "Let me go check on your shit. This date seems pretty important. It's all anyone around here has talked about. I figured you were a Kennedy or something. Anyway, you don't want to waste all your banter on me."

Hank disappeared into the kitchen and August resumed his waiting. He dug a pen out of his messenger bag and swiped a sticky note from the other side of the bar. He wrote Ruby a quick thank you and stuck it to the stack of papers on her table. Hank returned with a fat basket and a set of keys.

"What are those?"

"Ruby said she didn't want you to drop anything. And to fill it up when you brought it back. And if you fuck it up, don't bother coming back, she'll find you. Good luck."

"Thanks, Hank!" August said, grabbing the keys and the basket's handle. "And here I thought we were getting off on the wrong foot."

"Oh, we are," Hank said. "That was Ruby's good luck. Just part of the message. I don't care what happens."

"See you next time, then. Been a real pleasure."

It was a short drive from Branchhall to Astoria Park thanks to Ruby's refurbished 1980 Cadillac Seville. August parked in the lot closest to the appointed meeting spot. He saw a figure walking in circles near an oak tree. Behind her, a wide grass runway that led to Shore Boulevard and the East River. He took a deep breath as he gathered everything out of the backseat. He grew more nervous with every step, especially when he got close enough to see the pattern of her skirt. He couldn't see the print clearly, but he guessed either birds or flying hams. That made him imagine the "Flying Toasters" screensaver from back in the 1990s. He focused on that to stay calm. He was just thrilled and relieved she showed up.

"Someone waiting for me," August said, walking toward her. "That's quite the cause for celebration in my life."

"I really couldn't have brought anything?" Eleanor asked. "Look kind of sweaty and overburdened."

"There's no romance in having a woman bring something to a first date," August said.

"Personal hygiene is involved at least. Let me grab that, Eleanor said, tugging the thin, polka-dotted blanket out from August's arm before he could object. She spread it out, letting it flutter down to earth.

"Polka dots, huh?" she said, sitting down, watching him struggle to find a suitable landing spot for the basket.

"My mother gave it to me," August said. "That's what my father told me, anyway."

"That's cute. Are you close with your parents?"

"Don't you want to know what's in here?" August said, lying down on his side, fat drops of sweat clinging to his nose.

Eleanor tried not to roll her eyes at his evasion, but she had dated one too many writers. She did it as sweetly as possible since this was their first date.

"Let's hope it's all vegan-friendly and gluten-free," she said.

"You're kidding," August said, his chest deflating.

"I am. You may read me the menu."

August lurched into a crouch and opened one of the basket's flaps.

"Lightly toasted focaccia bread, tomato, the thinnest slice of Swiss cheese you'll ever see, pounded grilled chicken, a drizzle of balsamic and strawberry dressing, and an egg white."

"Damn, that sounds delicious. Do you have anything to wash all of this goodness down with?"

"Shit, I do, but I forgot something in the car. Hold on to this and don't run away."

Eleanor accepted the daisy August pulled out of the basket and held it to her nose like she was a Disney cartoon. Maybe if she played the clichéd smitten princess, she could peel away a few of his outer layers.

She watched as he ran to the parking lot. His form matched that of someone who had lived in the city his whole life. More like he was escaping something as opposed to lightheartedly jogging. Eleanor reminded herself that assuming a second date based on someone's ass violated some kind of feminist rule. She'd make sure he still earned it in some other way.

August returned holding two oversized wine glasses.

"Real glass," Eleanor said. "My goodness."

"People should stop using plastic drinkware when they turn thirty. In truth, well before that."

"Even on picnics?"

"Especially on picnics."

"And what goes in these?"

"Well, the Malbec I brought."

August lost his balance and dropped one of the glasses. It fell dully against the grass, but hard enough to crack in three places.

"Looks like we'll have to share," Eleanor said, stifling a giggle.

"I'm not a good sharer."

"Neither am I. But I can't have you drinking from the bottle like a lout. You know what would have prevented this?"

"Plastic drinkware."

"Yes! But the effort is noted and cataloged."

"Who talks like this?"

"If this bothers you, just wait until I break out the really theatrical characters in here," Eleanor said, wiggling her finger in a circle around her head. "Wine, please."

August recovered and poured out a generous amount of wine in the unscathed glass. He handed it to Eleanor as he unpacked the sandwiches.

"So did you make all this yourself?" she asked.

"I had a little help. I don't cook much," August said.

"Male incompetence?"

"Personal choice."

"Having something to do with some chauvinistic, white male pathos, I'm assuming?"

"Not everything about me has to do with being a writer."

"Do your tattoos mean something?"

"All ink has meaning."

"Favorite holiday?"

"Not one for holidays."

"What's your favorite color?"

"Hard to pick just one."

"Are you going to make me torture every answer out of you?"

"Yes," August said. "Try these homemade potato chips."

"Because none of that had to do with being a moody writer," Eleanor said, plucking a chip out of the plastic container in August's outstretched hand. "Homemade, huh?"

"Someone close to me is a little tired of me pursuing the wrong women. You drunkenly whine a few times and you're marked. Anyway, she wanted me to make a good impression. Sensed you could be different."

"And why would she think that?"

"That's what I told her."

"Ah, well, that's nice to hear. Sounds like a smart woman. Relative?"

"Something like that. Close enough, I guess."

Eleanor resolved to let him get away with a lot today. Who knew, maybe tomorrow she'd need him to forgive her for much more.

"Do I get to ask you questions now?" August asked.

"Oh, is this a game?"

"Sure."

"I mean, you ask one, I ask one. Until we exhaust everything we could possibly think of."

"Have a feeling that could take years for you."

"Very perceptive. I have questions for days."

"Can I get an answer to mine?"

"What did you ask again?"

"If I can ask you questions now."

"Oh. Yes. I'd love that."

"Where'd you grow up?"

"In a bar," Eleanor said, expecting August's eyebrows to rise in surprise.

"Me too," he said, tossing a chip up and catching it in his mouth.

"I find that hard to believe."

"More of a restaurant, really," August said. "But it has a bar. I have my own stool and everything."

"Last one on the corner?"

"Only when Bernie's not there. If she is, I'm the next one over."

"Our regular is named Lucinda."

"One of your parents work there?"

"My mom owns it. Well, owned it. Man, that's still weird to say. We still do an annual food drive. Always feels like home."

"What does she do now?"

"Lawyer."

August stopped himself from downing the last bite of his sandwich.

"Wait," he said. "She's not—"

"Afraid so."

"The curly-haired woman on the park benches, billboards, the Q46 ..."

"... and right field at Jack Kaiser Stadium at St. John's. Go Red Storm!"

"Wow."

"Intimidated? She's usually a third-date topic. Not that I've had a ton of third dates. Mainly because of the intimidation. Mine, I mean. She must have taught me well."

"I wasn't allowed to be intimidated by strong women."

"Assuming this pseudo-relative is the reason?"

"Yeah."

"Well, anyway, she went to night school while running the bar. Bought it from the owner when she earned enough money. She had me work there to build character, but I loved it. Most bars don't do well. Hers did. Of course, it did. She sold it when I graduated college. I worked summer breaks, but she didn't want me hanging around bartending with no other plans. She didn't have to worry. I'm very ambitious. And somewhat of a goody-two-shoes. I can admit it. But that's how she is. A plan gets in her head and that's that. It eventually gets into mine and ..."

"You talk a lot ..."

"Bad thing?

"... and I would have finished by saying I like it. You have a very pleasing speech pattern."

"That's not creepy at all."

"Sorry. May I try to make it up to you?"

"You may."

August reached back into the basket and pulled out a small cooler bag. He opened it and sifted through the loose ice cubes. He handed Eleanor a shot-glass-sized container and a spoon.

"No way," she said, opening the lid. She quickly dug her spoon into the pink and brown swirl. "Is this...?"

"Yep, made this morning," August said. "Sorry about the strawberry. Apparently, there was an excess."

"I like strawberries. I have to meet this woman."

"She'd like you."

"Really?"

"I don't know. I'm not convinced she likes me."

"No one who hates someone delivers a spread like this."

"Well, obligation tends to go a long way. What about your father?"

"He's more of a no-date topic. Besides, wasn't it my question?"

"Yes. I think you owe me a couple at this point."

"In that case, tell me something true about yourself."

"That's more of a statement. In fact, it *is* a statement."

"Yeah, but there was questioning intent. This will get old if you litigate everything I say."

"My favorite color is green."

"See? Easy."

"My turn," August said. "Would you consider going on another date with me?"

Eleanor finished her ice cream and put the container's lid back on. She brushed crumbs off her skirt (*plump cardinals*, August had noted) and took a deep breath.

"Why don't we leave it as we had a nice afternoon."

"Okay."

"Don't look so glum," she said, imagining him packing everything up and storming off. "I said afternoon. There's an entire evening to live through."

"Oh yeah?" August asked. "What did you have in mind?"

"It wasn't your question, but I have a plan. I hope you can take it because the real drinking and conversation is about to begin."

3.

Eleanor sat with her hangover in her lone kitchen chair, listening to the coffeemaker gurgle far too slowly.

She could smell August's cologne and feel the sticky vinyl from the booth they were ensconced in all night on her skin. Another night of too many cocktails and one-sided conversation. She shook as much out of him as possible before the bourbon took over. At that point, all she wanted to do was push him to the ground and shove her tongue in his mouth. This emotional roller coaster was as infuriating as it was intoxicating.

Two stern, heavy knocks on her front door shook the wine glasses hanging on a rack under her cabinets.

"Eleanor, it's your mother."

"Of course," Eleanor muttered. "Hang on, Mom, let me put on some effin' pants," she barked.

"Language, dear."

This from the defense attorney half the city fears, Eleanor thought.

She couldn't find the black pants she had flung off before getting in bed last night. She was sure they were in a tight, sweaty ball somewhere in this mess, but she didn't have the patience to hunt for them. Especially not with her mother waiting at the door. The knocking would resume soon enough. And more yelling. Chaste yelling, of course.

Eleanor decided to just wrap herself into the pink and yellow bathrobe August bought for her at the Rainbow on First Avenue in between 75th and 76th Streets. He had her try on the handful on the rack before she settled on this one. He washed it five times for her after she explained her phobia about buying clothing that wasn't shrink-wrapped or well attended by overbearing salespeople. Yet another gift from her mother's collection of neuroses she had passed down. Eleanor was still somewhat leery about remnant germs and bed bugs, but it was the softest item of clothing she owned. As an added bonus, it was sure to annoy her mother, who objected to anything not purchased at Neiman Marcus or some high-end SoHo boutique.

"Have you fallen down?" Eleanor's mother yelled, banging on the door three more times. "Do I need to find you medical attention?"

Eleanor skipped over to the door and unlocked the deadbolt.

"Finally," her mother said. "What *are* you wearing?"

"Good morning, Pearl," Eleanor said. "Please come in."

"I prefer when you call me Mom. And, seriously, has that thing been fumigated? It looks like you bought it at a tag sale following the owner's death from a long illness."

This wasn't the Pearl from the advertising. Her brown hair was down, brushed, but not straightened. Eleanor couldn't tell whether her mother was wearing black jeans or jeggings. Matching black flats, not heels, which meant she stood right at five feet. This had to be bad.

"Gift from August," Eleanor finally replied.

"Ah, yes, it looks like his taste. Is that still going on?"

"We had dinner at your house a week ago. So, yes."

"Been a few months, right?"

"We've dated longer than that. As you are also well aware. Can I offer you coffee or tea while you judge my life? A vial of blood, perhaps?"

"I'm okay," Pearl said. "Although that coffee does smell ... interesting."

"It's cheap, Mom," Eleanor said. "I don't even know what brand it is. Or if it has a brand. Might just be a rusted metal tin with coffee scribbled in Sharpie across the front. Can I take your jacket?"

"No, thank you. It's not that kind of visit."

"Then what kind is it?"

"A bad kind. At least initially. In time, you'll see it as a good one."

"So this is about me and August."

"Yes. You and August."

"A minute ago you weren't sure he existed, and now it's 'you and August.'"

"This is going to take a lot longer if you keep up the sarcasm."

"In that case, I better take your jacket."

"For goodness sake, Eleanor, you only have one chair. You can't be too attached. Where does he sit when he's here?"

"Not that I need to defend my relationship or anything, but one of the only times *I've* sat at this table was about five minutes before you walked in. What does it matter? He could stand or sit on my lap. Or sit on the toilet to eat for all I care. What does anything have to do with dating August? Or not dating him, according to your insinuations?"

"You will not end up with someone like your father. He's bound to leave you, whether or not he loves you. He's built for leaving. That's all he knows."

"You forced Dad to leave. I've heard the stories."

"Yes, and these are all the reasons why. Let this go as far as you want as long as you know it needs to end the right way. He's already in love with you, so it's going to be messy. I see the indecision in your eyes. Sooner is better, but you're a big girl. Have some more fun, if you wish."

"I think I'm past the age where you can tell me who I can and can't date."

"Not after all I've given you. Everything I've built to get you to this point. You're meant to go up in life. Far higher than myself."

"You're on buses, Mom. I don't want a public life."

"You're still young enough not to know what you want. Which is why things need to end with August. Eventually."

"You don't know anything about him."

"I don't know what's worse—you thinking there's more to this boy or that your rebuttals belong on a teenage soap opera."

"August is likely more ambitious than I am. He's driven. Relentlessly. Reminds me of someone else I know."

"There will always be a ceiling for him. How long is it going to take him to get to where you are? A decade? More? Then what kind of life are you going to have waiting for him? Or, worse, dragging him like an anchor across what could have been your future? Is that what you want? Don't you have any respect for yourself? Fighting with me like this over a boy? The sex can't be that worth—"

"Stop!" Eleanor shouted, jumping up on the balls of her feet. "Just stop. I'm not a jury. You don't have to make a closing argument about my relationship. *Relationship*. I don't know if that's even something you're capable of. What did we have all these years? Certainly wasn't loving. Purely transactional. Well, I'm canceling the partnership. Is there anything else, Mother?"

Pearl folded her hands in front of her for a moment. Eleanor dug her arms into the front pockets of the robe as far as they could go. The coffeemaker burped and then sighed a few more drops into the full pot.

"I know how much you value your freedom," Pearl said, reaching into her pocketbook. She took out a long white envelope that Eleanor could see was filled with bright green hundred-dollar bills. "I also know that freedom comes at a cost. A real one, not the imagined ones you pile up in your head to use against me. This contains a couple of months' rent. Whether or not you cut August loose, it's yours. Just a mother taking care of her daughter."

Pearl picked up Eleanor's empty coffee cup—which revealed starlings in flight when heated, another gift from August—and placed the envelope under it.

"A mother knows best," Pearl said as she walked toward the door. Eleanor's lungs deflated as she watched her mother open it and step over the threshold. Pearl was a sliver away from shutting the door when she poked her head back in, her eyes unblinking and serious.

"Always," she said.

Eleanor stood in the middle of her little apartment, watching the door close slowly without her mother's help. She heard her phone vibrate on the table. August texting her, exuberant as always after spending a night with her. She didn't dare move yet, convinced her mother's presence hadn't really left and would return for one last jab.

She waited five minutes, truly alone now. She walked over and fingered the assault on her independence wedged under her cup. She picked up her phone and looked at August's messages, all fifteen of them—and counting. In between sharing Bob Dylan and Bruce Springsteen lyrics that reminded him of her, he told her he loved her and that he was trying his best to open up. It wasn't easy for him, had never been because of who had left him and when, but she made him feel like it was possible. That she was the missing piece that would stay, that would make him want to stay.

Eleanor put her phone to sleep, feeling her mother's words killing any chance at joy, and said, "Oh, August ..."

194 DANIEL FORD

Acknowledgements

My Aunt Cathy passed away while I was writing this collection, and while she read my first novel, she never got to ask me all the questions (likely dealing with the sex and violence) she had about it. I sense she would have even more after reading *Black Coffee*, but be secretly thrilled she's the main character in the titular story. Thank you for continuing to inspire my storytelling, and we'll meet for coffee further down the road.

My wife's grandfather, known most affectionately as Pa Tony, passed away this past March. He was a wonderful man, and everyone who knew him loved him. Tony had a terrific sense of humor, and he had such impeccable comedic timing. So much so that he worked his way into my debut novel *Sid Sanford Lives!* Thanks for everything Tony, and don't be surprised if you show up in more of my fiction. Keys are on the counter and I'll take good care of Stephanie.

Thank you to all of the authors who so generously lent their time to reading and giving me great notes about these stories. Couldn't have done it without the help of Hank Phillippi Ryan, Phoef Sutton, Bianca Marais, Drew Yanno, Daniel Paisner, Grayson Morley, Edwin Hill, Nicole Blades, James Tate Hill, Giano Cromley, Calder G. Lorenz, and Steph Post, Gary Almeter, and Joseph Passanisi. Special thanks to my long-lost Jewish brother and Paul Simon-loving wordsmith Spencer Wise.

Thanks to Rich Dalglish for his samurai sword, which has been honing my words since I was a young cub at *JCK magazine*. Speaking of *JCK* cohorts, thanks to Cristina Cianci for lending her photography skills and for testing out promotional cocktails.

Thank you to all my beta readers, including Dave Pezza, Paul Lenzi, Ross Foniri, Rachel Tyner, Caitlin Malcuit, David Herder, Charlie Keating, Catherine Kearns, Jocelyn Wheaton, Mike Nelson, and everyone else I bothered with questions about tone, style, and grammar.

Thanks to Sean Tuohy and the rest of the Writer's Bone crew. We added three podcasts while I was writing this, and, instead of killing me, it inspired me even more. Thanks to Mark Jordan Legan, Jennifer Keishin Armstrong, and Kimberly Potts for those never-ending email chains that always make me laugh. Special thanks to Phoef Sutton for adding his Emmy-winning eyes to several stories and his boundless enthusiasm for the craft.

Thank you to the Ford, Blanchette, Schaefer, Brannen, Galayda, Dietrich, and D'Angelo families for being supportive of my work and still talking to me after you found out what I've been writing about all these years. Special thanks to Rory, the little lion, for adding a much-needed spark to get this collection across the finish line. When you decide to rebel in your teens, our door is always open. A very special thanks to Karen Schaefer, mother-in-law of the century, for so many cups of coffee and conversation.

The real key to this whole writing thing is finding a partner that not only loves and supports you, but also pries you away from the black hole of despair you can occasionally get mired in. Stephanie, thank you for marrying me, adding the sunlight to every room and park we're in, supplying the perfect witty response when I need it most, and penning wonderful new chapters to our love story every day. More adventures ahead!

About the Author

Daniel Ford is the author of *Sid Sanford Lives!* He also co-hosts Writer's Bone, a literary podcast dedicated to championing aspiring authors and screenwriters. Ford lives with his wife Stephanie in Boston's North End, where coffee and cannoli are always within arm's reach. Find more of his work at danielfford.com.

Excerpt from *Sid Sanford Lives*!

And you thought Sid Sanford wouldn't make an appearance in a short story collection inspired by his favorite caffeinated beverage? Ha!

Not writing for a character I've become so identified with on the page and in real life was both daunting and cathartic. There were times crafting August and Eleanor or Mike from "343" that I wished I had Sid around to torture for a few more paragraphs. He bent into whatever form I needed without complaint or resentment.

I haven't closed the door on returning to Sid's world, but he certainly needs the rest and there are more characters and plots to explore in the meantime. Pour one more cup of coffee and enjoy this excerpt from my debut novel.

* * *

Constance's question made Sid drop the diner's oversized menu in his lap.

"What?" he asked.

"So do you have a girlfriend?" she asked again.

Sid rubbed the back of his head, took a breath, and looked her right in the eyes.

"Sort of," he said.

"You're going to need to explain that one."

Constance tried not to sound prosecutorial, however, the guy sitting across from her smelled like a distillery and had whined about the long bus ride to Astoria.

Sid opened his mouth and shut it again. He let out a short, nervous laugh. He rubbed the back of his head again. Constance saw sweat beading up along his hairline.

"Do you know what you want, sweetie?" the waitress asked.

"Well, I know one of us does," she said.

They both ordered a coffee and got back to staring each other down. The waitress had given him a moment to regroup and Constance could see he had taken full advantage of it. His eyes were as clear as they had been all night, his hands were folded calmly on the table in front of him, and he appeared like he was ready to talk honestly.

"I'm single," he said. "I have a good friend in Connecticut, she's family really, and we have a relationship that defies explanation. We've never really been on the same page at the same time, and probably never will be. And you know what, I think both of us have made some kind of peace with that and our friendship has been better for it recently. 'Sort of' was a poor choice of words. If I had a girlfriend, I wouldn't be here tonight. I'm not that kind of person. I'm a good guy."

"Do you love her?"

"I'm not in love with her."

"But you do love her."

"Of course I do."

"And you don't think that would be a problem when you start dating someone else?"

"You don't think someone can love a person without being in love with them?"

"I do, but you didn't answer the question."

"I'm content with the expectations for that relationship, and know that it won't affect any relationship that comes along."

"Are you running for office?"

"I've heard that before."

"I bet you have."

The waitress brought their coffees. Constance reached over to grab the sugar and cream, but Sid brushed her hand away and held the cream container over her cup.

"Tell me when," he said.

"That's your plan to get back into my good graces? Has this ever worked for you before?"

He laughed, causing his hand to shake. Cream spilled down the side of the white cup and puddled into the saucer.

"I figured what better way to impress a coffee-loving New Yorker than to find out how she takes her coffee," Sid said.

"I didn't tell you to stop," Constance said.

"Seriously?"

"Yes."

"Should we get you a bigger cup so you can have a little coffee with your cream?"

"Funny. Keep pouring."

"You got it."

Constance watched as he continued his mission. She nodded when she was satisfied. She handed him two sugar packets. He dumped them in and clanged the spoon up against the sides of the cup as he stirred everything together. He slid the saucer closer to her and bowed. She applauded.

"So, what do you want to know about me?" Sid asked.

"I'll decide whether I want to know anything more about you after I determine how good a job you did on my coffee," Constance said, blowing across the surface of her drink.

"Of course, take your time. Don't hold back your judgment."

"I think you know by now that's not my style."

"This is true."

Constance finally touched her lips to the cup and took a small sip.

"Okay, you pass."

"That's it?"

"Yup."

"No other observations, comments, concerns? I just pass?"

"Don't push it."

"You got it."

Sid rubbed the back of his head. Constance couldn't help being fascinated by the boy in front of her. She really believed he was being genuine at this point.

"How do you know I love coffee?" Constance asked.

"You always have one in class."

"It's my first class of the day, I could just need the energy."

"Yeah, there's more to it than that."

"Such as..."

"It's just how you drink it."

"And how do I drink it exactly?"

"I don't know."

"You've been creepily watching me drink coffee for weeks and don't know exactly how I drink it?"

"It's hard for me to take my eyes off of you."

Constance put her head down and tried to hide the smile that had burst onto her face like a child's soap bubble on a summer day.

"That is sweet," she said. "Thank you."

"You're welcome."

"You certainly have a way with words, Sid Sanford."

"God, I hope so, I want to be a writer when I'm all growed up."

"Me too."

"Well, why do you want to be a writer?"

Constance thought of all the notebooks she had stacked up in her closet. Notebooks she had written in since she was a little girl, notebooks that were yellowed and faded in spots, notebooks that she had never shown anyone outside of her immediate family. Some contained scribbles and rambling thoughts, while others contained fully formed story ideas in various stages of completion. She often looked to them when she needed a spark of creative inspiration. She wanted to be a writer because that's all she'd ever done and all she ever wanted to do. She was good at it and wanted to improve on a daily basis.

"That's a great answer," he said.

She hadn't realized she'd been talking out loud.

"Too much information for a first date?" she asked.

"Not at all. Exactly the answer I was hoping for. I'm the same way. I wasn't an athlete, I wasn't the smartest kid in the class, and I didn't have the sense of humor to be the class clown. Writing has been the only thing I've ever been good at, so I figured majoring in journalism in New York City was a no brainer."

She loved that he was tripping over his words telling her this. It was as if his mouth couldn't keep up with the passionate thoughts.

"I was going to ask you about that. How does a Connecticut boy like you end up in the big city?" she asked. "You didn't want to stay close to home?"

"I've been in love with the city since my mother took me to the Radio City Christmas Spectacular when I was nine years old," he answered. "My life's goal from that point on was to live here. Besides, practically my entire high school went to UCONN. If I had stayed, I would have never left home."

"Did part of you leave because of your complicated relationship with your best friend?"

Sid shrugged.

"That's a yes," Constance said.

"That's an 'I don't know, I've never thought of it that way before.' Maybe, but my love for New York City outweighed every other consideration."

"Fair enough. Do you miss your family?"

Sid pursed his lips tightly. He looked down, seemingly looking deep into the coffee that was no longer in his cup.

"It's okay, you don't have to answer," Constance said. "I didn't mean to make you sad."

"I miss them all terribly. I love my family," he said. "I don't know why they put up with me, but they do."

"Do you consider yourself a good man?"

"I like to think so. I do try. I can't say I've made a lot of smart decisions since I've been here or before that, but my parents hammered a good soul into me. I guess it's just about being young right now and accepting that fact rather than rebelling against it."

"Aren't you going to ask me if I think I'm a good person?" Constance asked.

"I don't need to," Sid said. "What's after dinner?"

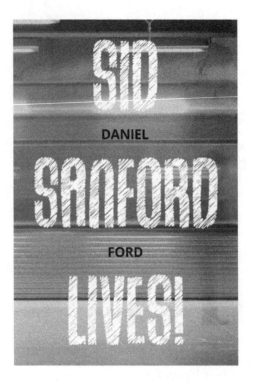

Available for purchase at 5050press.com.

Priscilla's Revolver

For *Sid Sanford Lives!*, my good friend Paul Lenzi distilled a specialty cocktail he called "S!d's Madhattan." A few precious fingers still exist in bottles skulking in the back of our refrigerators.

For *Black Coffee*'s signature cocktail, I consulted my literary friend Sam Slaughter, author of *Are You Afraid of the Dark Rum?*, who approved San Francisco bartender Jon Santer's twist on a Manhattan. Once Priscilla appeared on the page in "Unkind Bud" there was no other choice for its name. Drop the needle on the *Black Coffee* playlist (which you can find on Spotify or on danielfford.com) and imbibe!

Priscilla's Revolver

- 2 oz. bourbon
- 1/2 oz. coffee liqueur
- 2 dashes orange bitters

Combine all ingredients in cocktail shaker or mixer.

Add ice and stir.

Strain into a classy cocktail glass of your choice.

Add orange peels to your heart's content.

Coming Soon from 50/50 Press

August Booker left the FBI for a teaching position at a small private college in Berksville, NY. Content teaching Criminology, he is pressured into helping the local police investigate a gruesome murder. He has one condition: it must be a learning experience for his three brightest students.

Sarah Rime just transferred to Upstate NY. On her first day she lands a murder investigation that has the little town in a frenzy. As if that wasn't enough pressure, the headstrong cop has to drag along a professor, a cheerleader, a computer jockey, and a senior citizen. Sounds like the beginning to a bad joke.

Will this unlikely team be able to find the killer before it happens again?

212 DANIEL FORD

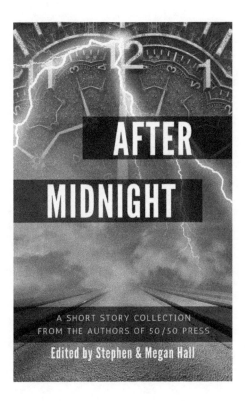

After Midnight is a compilation of amazing stories by some of the most creative authors of 50/50 Press. The proceeds go to Literacy New York of the Greater Capital Region. The nonprofit organization helps both English speakers and English Language Learners with reading, writing, and oral communication. They have a network of volunteers throughout four counties who tutor and teach classes to help adults with literacy needs.

You can read more about them
here: https://www.literacynycap.org/programs

CPSIA information can be obtained
at www.ICGtesting.com
Printed in the USA
LVHW091343181019
634641LV00001B/1/P